Three

Georges Simenon

Translated by David Carter

ET REMOTISSIMA PROPE

Modern Voices

Modern Voices
Published by Hesperus Press Limited
4 Rickett Street, London SW6 1RU
www.hesperuspress.com

Three Crimes first published in French as *Les trois crimes des mes amis* in 1938
First published by Hesperus Press Limited, 2006

Les trois crimes de mes amis © 1938 Georges Simenon Ltd, a Chorion Company. All rights reserved.
Introduction and English language translation © David Carter, 2006

Designed and typeset by Fraser Muggeridge studio
Printed in Jordan by the Jordan National Press

ISBN: 1-84391-421-2
ISBN13: 978-1-84391-421-1

All rights reserved. This book is sold subject to the condition that it shall not be resold, lent, hired out or otherwise circulated without the express prior consent of the publisher.

Contents

Introduction vii

Three Crimes 1
  Notes 127

Biographical note 129

Introduction

He acquired a reputation for excess: one of the world's most prolific writers and, by his own account, one of its most promiscuous lovers. At the height of his fame over 500 million copies of Georges Simenon's books were sold all over the world in fifty-five languages. Scholars still argue about the precise number of books he wrote, but there are at least 230 works in his own name, many still not translated into English, and a further 200 under various pseudonyms. Concerning the number of his lovers, he once declared casually, in an almost offhand way, that he had probably had sexual relations with about 10,000 women since the age of thirteen. This revelation occurred in an interview he was conducting shortly after his seventy-fourth birthday in 1977, with his old friend, the Italian film director Federico Fellini. They were discussing Fellini's new film *Casanova*.

His work has been admired by some of the most famous writers of the twentieth century: Jean Anouilh, Henry Miller, Somerset Maugham, John Cowper Powys, T.S. Eliot, Thornton Wilder and many others, most famously by André Gide, who described him as 'the most genuine novelist we have had in literature'. Numerous films have been based on his books, by such directors as Jean Renoir, Claude Chabrol, Henry Hathaway, Patrice Leconte and Bertrand Tavernier. Most famous of all perhaps have been the many television series, in various languages, based on his novels about the pipe-smoking, intuitive, French police chief, Jules Maigret.

Biographers of Simenon have had to grapple with the many contradictions between established facts and Simenon's own accounts of his life. He wrote four actual biographies and, after he decided to stop writing novels, he dictated twenty-two volumes of memoirs, but they require critical reading and careful checking of facts.

It is certain, however, that he was born in Liège, Belgium, on 12th February 1903, in a devout Catholic family. The wartime occupation of Liège by the Germans led Simenon to realise that in order to survive he had to deceive and cheat people, and he spent more time on the town than at school. He got his first job in 1919 as an office boy and then became a junior reporter for the *Gazette de Liège*. When not working he led a very Bohemian lifestyle, and it is this that is depicted in the work *Les trois crimes de mes amis* ('*The Three Crimes of my Friends*'), translated here as *Three Crimes*, and first published in 1938. This and *Pedigree* (1948) are the two most closely autobiographical of Simenon's novels, for novels he considered them to be, and not autobiographies. Nevertheless all the details in *Three Crimes* come directly from his own experience, including the names of all the characters. The work is novelistic, however, in its evocation and dramatisation of situations and events.

The work was written after he had already published nineteen Maigret novels and during a period when he was considering writing no more about the famous chief inspector, but was devoting himself to his more harrowing novels, which he preferred to call '*romans durs*'. Nine of these novels were published in the same year as *Three Crimes*, including one that many regard as one of his masterpieces, *The Man Who Watched the Trains Go By*, and a year before another recognised masterpiece, *Chez Krull*. In *Three Crimes* he looked back at formative experiences in his own youth, at a period in his own life when he was a companion to men who were to become criminals. It was a path he might well have taken himself, had he not turned to writing novels about such men. As he writes in the opening chapter of *Three Crimes*: 'The three crimes of my friends resemble all the crimes that I have related.'

Simenon's title is a little misleading and the scope of the work is broader than it suggests. There are in fact four serious crimes related in the work, and several lesser ones. Four people are murdered, but there are also several instances of blackmail, as well as the seduction of under-age girls. The four serious crimes are committed by two of Simenon's acquaintances, the eccentric bookseller and dabbler in dark arts, Hyacinthe Danse, and the flamboyant journalist and pimp, Ferdinand Deblauwe. Simenon arrived at his total of three crimes by conflating two of them. Deblauwe murdered his mistress' lover, and Danse murdered first his mistress and then his mother, and finally his former Jesuit confessor, who had also been Simenon's teacher. He murdered his mistress and his mother in quick succession, so that it is this event that Simenon considers to be one crime. Details of these crimes are indicated in the first chapter, so that there is no mystery to be solved. As with most of Simenon's writing it is the why and the how of any crime that fascinates.

The fates of other individuals are intertwined with those of Simenon, Danse and Deblauwe. There is the mysterious Fakir, who reads palms and practises hypnotism, and Kleine, Little K..., the poor artist, who, after being put into a state of catalepsy by the Fakir, is carried off to his room by Simenon, only to be found the next morning hanging from the portal of the church of Saint-Pholien. And there are the 'Two Brothers', involved in various nefarious dealings, who drive their mother to sell her own clothes to support them.

The style of the work reflects very closely Simenon's concerns in writing it. He becomes obsessed with the possible inter-relationships between the fates of individuals, and with the likelihood that these fates are all in some mysterious way inevitable. He speculates about motives and feelings but draws no conclusions. This is reflected in the frequent use of unanswered questions and unfinished sentences ending in an ellipsis. These are devices he uses in many of his works, but in this work more so than in most. He changes tenses frequently and abruptly, so that a memory often seems to change to lived experience and back again within the space of a few sentences. He never lets the reader forget the outcomes of the events he retells, and forces one to concentrate on each step in the process. As with all his writing Simenon refrains from moral judgement and seems to view the events finally through the eyes of his own grandmother at the end of the book, whose favourite comment on all strange human behaviour was 'The things people do!'

Simenon was to draw on the experiences of this rather wanton period of his youth in Liège in several of his works, most notably in the second Maigret novel, *Le pendu de Saint-Pholien* (1931), translated as *The Crime of Inspector Maigret*, and also as *Maigret and the Hundred Gibbets*. A close translation of the original title makes the connection with *Three Crimes* very clear: 'The Hanged Man of Saint-Pholien'. In this novel Maigret discovers a connection between a suicide and a mysterious group of individuals in Liège, who call themselves 'The Companions of the Apocalypse'. The group is clearly modelled on the group to which Simenon belonged, styling itself the '*caque*'. In the novel a young man is murdered and another is found hanging from the portal of the church of Saint-Pholien. This character is clearly based on Simenon's friend Kleine (renamed Klein in the novel). The description of the group's meeting place is very similar to that in the third chapter of *Three Crimes*:

> ... in one corner, there was a kind of divan, or rather a spring mattress, partly covered with a piece of cretonne. Just above it dangled an odd-shaped lantern, with coloured glass, the sort sometimes to be seen in junk shops.
>
> Sections of an incomplete skeleton, the kind used by students, had been flung down on the divan.

And there are inscriptions around, such as 'Long live Satan, grandfather of the world', and 'Welcome to the Damned' (*Maigret and the Hundred Gibbets*, Penguin, 1963). One is tempted to think that Simenon was writing to purge himself of his own sense of guilt concerning the death of Little K…

The two strange solitary individuals that Simenon refers to at the beginning of chapter eight of *Three Crimes* have also found their literary realisation in one of Simenon's most accomplished novels, *Monsieur Hire's Engagement* (1933): 'At two o'clock he was doing up parcels again. At half past three he was writing addresses on labels, and about four o'clock he began sticking the labels on the parcels.'

Even Monsieur Hire's classified advertisement is similar: 'Eighty to a hundred francs a day for easy work without leaving present employment…' (*Monsieur Hire's Engagement* in *The Sacrifice*, Hamish Hamilton, 1956).

Three Crimes cannot be rated as one of Simenon's most accomplished works, but it does provide vivid insight into the period of Simenon's youth during the latter part of the First World War and just after. There are memorable evocations of life in Liège under the German occupation and of street scenes in German towns during the period of hyperinflation, when Belgians flocked over the border to buy cheap goods. It is also enjoyable to perceive how Simenon gently mocks his younger self.

I have endeavoured to evoke as closely as possible the characteristics of Simenon's prose in my translation, retaining his use of short paragraphs and incomplete sentences followed by ellipses. I have also been faithful to his use of exclamation marks. It has been necessary however on occasions to break up some of his longer rambling sentences, which are otherwise difficult to render coherently in English. The French convention of using dashes to indicate dialogue has been replaced by quotation marks. All the sequences in capitals reflect Simenon's usage.

Enormous gratitude is due to several friends whose opinions I sought on obscure and difficult aspects of the French language. Some devoted much time and effort to helping me. Responsibility for the final decisions is of course mine alone. I do not wish to weigh their contributions against each other and so list their names alphabetically: Philippe Blanvillain, Annie Edwards, Alan Miles, Philip and Bénédicte Morris and Gilles Pinard. Finally, special thanks are due to Katherine Venn for her meticulous editing.

– David Carter, 2006

Three Crimes

I

It's puzzling! A little while ago, I mean, just a moment ago, as I was writing my title, I was convinced that I was going to start my story, just as you start a novel, and the only difference would consist in its being true.

Now, all of a sudden I realise what is artificial about a novel, what makes it impossible for it ever to be an image of life: *a novel has a beginning and an end!*

Hyacinthe Danse killed his mistress and his mother on 10th May, 1933. But when did the crime really begin? Was it when he was publishing the magazine *Nanesse* in Liège, of which I, by an unlikely chance, became one of the founders, at the age of seventeen? Was it when, together with Deblauwe, we were wandering around the town streets? Wasn't it a long time before that, during the war, when girls would whisper to us that, behind the closed shutters of a certain bookshop…

And Deblauwe? When was it that he started to become a murderer? And the Fakir? Why was it just yesterday that I learned that he had died in a hospital in Paris, died of poverty, of alcoholism, of all kinds of vile diseases, and all kinds of vices and defects, one of those deaths about which one is forewarned many days beforehand by their stench.

Why? How? Where should one begin, since there is no beginning, nor any other link, over the years and across space, between three crimes, between five or six deaths and between a handful of the living, except for myself?

I seem to hear Danse's voice, in the strange Court of the Assizes in Liège, pounding out the words, 'When I was four years old my mother took me to the countryside, and there, in a farmyard, I saw a man killing a sow, first with a hammer, and then by slitting its throat…'

When he was four years old, I did not know him; I wasn't even born. What is more, I wasn't there when, forty years later, in a small house in the French countryside, he killed his mother and his mistress in exactly the same way he had once seen a sow being killed.

More pertinently, could I say at what moment Little K..., whose shoes let water, decided to hang himself from the door of the church of Saint-Pholien? And, a few hours before this act, hadn't I been carrying him on my back, inert from having drunk too much, and still dribbling after having vomited everything that had been in his body?

Three crimes! It's easily said. But *before* them?

I remember that, when I was very young, I devoured novels at the rate of three a day, and they all left me dissatisfied. Having read the last page I would just sigh.

'But then what?'

Why did it finish, since all the characters weren't dead? Why did the author decide like that, at will and gratuitously, that all of a sudden there would be nothing more but a white page with the name of the printer?

Nowadays it is not the ending that bothers me, but the beginning. What right do I have to present a thirty-five-year-old Deblauwe as if he had never existed before? And what about the others as well, whom I only knew at a given moment in their lives, as though they were passing by?

And what about that link I was talking about... One scene I remember, in 1915... And another, two years later, while I was trying out my first pair of long trousers... Danse... Deblauwe... Then the Fakir and Little K...

I did not suspect anything, and my friends were murderers! I did not suspect anything a few years later when I started to write detective novels, that is to say stories about false crimes. In the meantime those people who had formerly been a part of my life, who had breathed the same atmosphere as me, shared the same pleasures, the same amusements, and discussed the same topics, were definitely starting to kill, one in the rue de Maubeuge, gunning a man down with a hail of bullets through the pocket of his gabardine coat, the other at Boullay, far from the place where he was born, and where he had lived. He was surrounded by French country people who were strangers to him, which perhaps drove him the following day to return to Liège, to wander round the familiar streets, and then kill at point blank range, with all the bullets in his cylinder, a Jesuit father who had been his confessor and mine.

Isn't it strange that, during this time, I, myself, was writing detective novels in which I was doing my best to create criminals?

Perhaps it is less strange than it seems, if one looks at it more closely, if one reads more attentively, for then what you find again in my books, besides very little imagination, are the settings, atmospheres and states of mind, which, for the other three, were bound to end in...

The three crimes of my friends resemble all the crimes that I have related. Only, due to the fact that they are true, and that I know their perpetrators, it is possible for me to write: 'He killed because...'

Because of nothing! Because of everything! At certain moments I think I understand everything and it seems to me that, in a few words, I will be able to...

But no! A moment later this truth that I touched upon almost vanishes into thin air and I see again a different Deblauwe, and a smiling, plump Danse behind his counter. I hear a phrase... Or it is the characteristic lingering odour of the Fakir, which rises up in my throat and I think I am wandering under the lamps daubed with blue in the wartime.

It is impossible to relate truths in an orderly and clear way: they will always appear less plausible than a novel.

It would be necessary to conjure up the entire German occupation, because I believe that it left its mark on the young people subjected to it just as profoundly as, a few years later, inflation was to leave its mark on a generation of Germans.

But it is even less possible to describe the occupation than it is inflation. It is not a question of facts: it's an ambience, a state of being, the smell of the barracks on the streets, the moving blotch of unfamiliar uniforms, marks replacing francs in your pockets, and the worry about eating taking the place of all other worries. It's new words and unknown pieces of music, mobile kitchens along the pavements, and the eye's habit of looking out for the new notice on the walls, which will specify from what time it is forbidden to be out and about, or which will announce a delivery of sugar at the 'supply store', unless it is to remind men older than eighteen years of their duty to report each week to the Kommandantur,[1] or, if the notice is a red one, it will list the names of the recently shot civilians…

Of course life continues and you have to get to school on time, learn your lessons, and do your homework, even if, in the break time, it means discussing a schoolmate whose father sells butter to the Germans or another whose mother has been seen with an officer of the Uhlans.[2]

The concerns of a thirteen-year-old kid remain with him forever, with others just added on. So, among a group of second-year pupils under the main staircase someone murmurs, 'My father managed to buy ten kilos of wheat at a farm. He was almost caught coming back into town…' Or else: 'The French have won a battle. My parents know about it from someone who crossed the Dutch border and who brought back a newspaper…'

The fact is that the main question above all concerns the girls in the school next door, and certain matters that some do not know very much about yet, but that others claim to know about and also to have actually achieved, and it also concerns the fact that, for a whole month, one class has been deeply disturbed by a cracked and yellowed erotic photograph in which you can see exactly how it is done.

The thousands of soldiers marching by, going up to and returning from the front, have terrible pangs of hunger, and, on the walls, posters refer to them crudely: 'Any woman who has had relations with a soldier and not had a medical...'

There are also details concerning the precautions that need to be taken. The streets are dark. For fear of air raids shop windows are not lit up, and a thick coat of blue paint makes the light of the gas lamps seem illusory.

The rue Féronstrée is a narrow street swarming with people, which the trams, narrowly missing the inadequate pavements, fill with their din.

This is where, in a second-hand bookshop, I used to buy and sell back my school books. There was a window full of them, arranged according to school. Ours were written by Jesuit fathers, and in the next window gaudier covers were spread out, which we did not dare to stop in front of, for fear of attracting the smile of a passer-by.

In fact, while supplying most of the secondary school pupils, Hyacinthe Danse also specialised in so-called saucy works, and at the back of his shop, I remember having noticed a shelf of 'flagellation', which amazed me.

The second-hand bookseller was an enormous chap, weighing about 130 kilos and whose rosy face always wore a cheerful smile. On Monday he would buy your manual of literature by R.P. Verrest off you for two marks and on Thursday he would sell it back to you for six marks, with a laugh and a friendly pat on the shoulder.

I must have been thirteen and a half years old and I was certainly in serious need of money when I decided one day to sell three books, which a friend had given me. They were three sumptuously bound volumes of Victor Hugo, which, as I found confirmed in the dictionary,[3] were part of the original edition.

I can see him now fiddling with them, and me facing him, hoping to hear him state an enormous figure.

I can see him putting the old books on the counter and pulling a filthy wallet out of his pocket, still full of one-mark bank notes.

'How much?' I asked, with a lump in my throat.

'Twenty marks the lot, my boy.'

'Never! It's the original edition, the Brussels one, and the binding alone…'

'Do you want twenty marks?'

'No! I'd rather keep the books.'

Why did he put himself between me and the books? Was he going to prevent me from taking them back?

'I said twenty marks… Now, I'm going to add something else: it would probably be unwise for you to go the rounds of second-hand booksellers with these books… But I'm a good chap…'

'What are you trying to say?'

'That your Victor Hugo volumes come from the university library… I'm not asking you anything… It doesn't concern me.'

I had turned scarlet and I don't know how the twenty one-mark notes passed from Danse's hand to mine. He saw me to the door and, when I turned round, I saw him on the doorstep, his hands in his pockets, his paunch protruding, and with his fat satisfied face.

I don't know if the occupation and the war have something to do with it, or if the first initiations into love always have this confused and furtive aspect.

My memories, I don't know why, are only memories of winter, of rain or drizzle, or fog, and I see again that long street, with its lamps painted blue, where from seven o'clock in the evening we would wander about for hours in almost total darkness, so that we got into the habit of taking along a pocket torch.

In Liège this promenade is called Le Carré,[4] for no reason, since you can walk endlessly from one end of the street to the other, meeting the same people twenty times in one evening.

We were the youngest there. I suppose that the prostitutes were not particularly pleased at having to do their work while we were running around after girls of our own age and sometimes sticking electric torches under their noses.

We were all poorly fed, both them and us, and poorly clothed too. And during one period we had nothing more than shoes with wooden soles.

The first cinemas were showing the Gribouille[5] films with a piano accompaniment and they sprayed the canvas screen in each interval.

There could be no question of hotel rooms, and, to tell the truth, they were not necessary.

Our initiations took place in corners with clothes soaked by the rain, thighs, the warmth of which one discovered suddenly under the ice-cold raincoat, and mouths, which tried to create some pleasure through kissing but which only managed to achieve it in theory.

'What did she say to you?'

'I swore not to repeat it.'

'Tell me! Only me... I won't tell it to anyone...'

We could hardly see each other and our clumsy hands were all the more determined for that.

'Tell me!'

How old were those girls? Fourteen? Fifteen? They were common little girls who came in groups and walked by in front of the men, laughing, but it was a laughter rooted in fear. We boys did not count for them. They had their secrets with which they made our mouths water.

'In any case, I wouldn't let myself be pushed around... And what is more she wouldn't dare go home...'

'Why?'

'I can't say... It concerns very serious matters...'

And naive as we were, we insisted for eight whole days on sharing the famous secret, which our girl friends never stopped chatting about between themselves.

'It's in a bookshop...'

'Which bookshop?'

'I'm not saying... He's got a card from the Kommandantur...'

'Who?'

'He has! That man! He has the right to arrest all the women on the street and take them off...'

'Why?'

'To make sure that they are healthy...'

Just that word alone! How it could shatter us!

'Is he a doctor?'

'No. But he visits them anyway... Damn! I've already said too much...'

And we passed on our miserable bits of information to each other, boasting that we had done much more in that way than we had actually done.

'I know who it is... It's Danse, the second-hand bookseller in the rue Féronstrée...'

'The one I sell my books to?'

Always that long dark street, with its closed shutters, its blue gas lamps, which had become our entire universe, with its furtive shadows, the soldiers you could recognise by the sound of their boots, and sometimes the prestigious grey cape of an officer passing rapidly by, the jangling of his spurs, and the perfume of a well-dressed woman...

'Sidonie had to be taken to hospital...'

'What's wrong with her?'

'It's not something that concerns men…'

They were odd girls, coming back to us, with a patronising manner, after having spent several mysterious hours in the company of real men who took them to eat in a restaurant!

'Yesterday, there were four girls… He planted a candle on a death's head…'

And Sidonie, who had gone there several times and who, due to being anaemic, gave me the impression of being a madonna, would purse her lips and wrap a fur collar, peeling all over, tightly round her neck.

'What did he do to you? Tell me!…'

The man was definitely Hyacinthe Danse, the one who bought our books off us and sold them back to us again with such a jovial manner. One of us had actually seen him entering the Kommandantur. And it was true that he had a card with German stamps on it, and also true that in the evening he used to stop young girls in the street and take them into his shop with its shutters closed.

It was also true that Sidonie had had to be taken to hospital. It was true that…

We ended up knowing about things bit by bit, but what the girls refused to tell us was what exactly he did to their little underdeveloped bodies.

'He isn't like the others… He's a lecherous…'

So that we deliberately went to look at Danse's shop, telling ourselves that in that old armchair, for example, in the evening, once when the shutters were lowered…

I can still hear the hoarse voice of a little girl, the daughter of a fruit and vegetable merchant:

'You shouldn't have let it happen!'

'He would've denounced me to the Germans…'

Fifteen years old? Fifteen and a half? Now I was wearing men's trousers and smoking a pipe with a thin stem. Suddenly, new uniforms appeared in the town, tired faces, shifty-looking figures: Russian prisoners, who the Germans were starting to set free, as they sensed the advent of their downfall.

'Who hasn't got their Russian?'

Every household wanted one. Every young girl was taking one for a walk around the town. They had suffered so much. And then one afternoon, we were in a huge music hall, and a comedian had just been singing: 'Caroline, pom, pom, pom, pom… She is ill, pom, pom, pom, pom…'. Then, I assure you, the same comedian, who must have gone mad, puts on a French uniform in the wings, a real one, comes back onto the stage and…

We could not believe that it was real. He sang '*La Marseillaise*', '*La Brabançonne*', and '*La Madelon*',[6] foreign tunes that we no longer knew.

And between the couplets he yelled: 'The war is over! The armistice has been signed!…'

It is true that there were still Germans wandering around the town. An interminable line of lorries, big guns, mobile kitchens and weary people stretched away to the east and the officers were tearing off their badges.

I don't know what Danse was doing while we were doing the farandole with strangers, both men and women, and while other groups were stripping women in the streets, who had had relations with the occupying troops, and were shaving their heads.

'The Allies are fifty kilometres away…'

Then, while they were about it, they ransacked the shops suspected of having done business with the enemy, and wardrobes with mirrors flew out of the windows, and hams cluttered up the gutters, while the police, who were powerless, contented themselves with repeating, 'Destroy them, but don't steal anything!'

I did not know K…yet, a nervous adolescent, more undernourished than anyone else, who followed the courses at the Academy of Painting while he was in secondary school.

What I do know is that he had also been so hungry that he had eaten swedes instead of potatoes, and that no doubt he wandered around in the evening like me, in the darkness of Le Carré, after the young girls.

He was the son of a worker in the suburbs. His mother was dead. He wanted to become a great artist.

On Armistice Day, he also took part in the farandole, which went into all the little cafés, getting free drinks, until everyone was giddy.

A detail: I happened to have on my arm a common girl with two rings on one of her fingers... Suddenly her mother catches sight of us, comes towards us, looks at me suspiciously, takes the rings from her daughter and moves away murmuring, 'You never know!...'

As for Danse, I now know what he was doing that evening, behind his lowered shutters. Danse was writing. He was composing an ode to peace, in the same room where the little girls...

'The Allies are twenty kilometres away...'

We went by bike to see them, advancing in columns, while another column made its way miserably towards the German frontier and the defeated officers were publicly kicked by their own men.

Danse was still working, in a frenzy, because at that time everything was done in a frenzy, the whole world was in a frenzy, overcome with giddiness, at the thought of something new.

'The Allies are in the inner suburbs...'

Danse was ready. His ode was finished. And in addition he had written some patriotic songs, which, without wasting a minute, he would be able to sing in the small towns, dressed in a crimson pre-war uniform, with his fat rosy face and a smile in his heart in accordance with the tradition of the genre.

In Paris, a certain Deblauwe, the son of an honourable owner of a hardware shop in Liège, was working in the rue Montmartre for a small newspaper, where he did stories about dogs that had got run over.

And up there in Montmartre, the Fakir, a man with greasy grey hair, from God knows what land in the Levant, went on his round of the cafés every evening, sat down in front of his clients and read the lines in their palms to them.

As for me, I got plastered for the first time in my life, still on the arm of the young girl whose mother had taken away her rings.

Could I have suspected that one year later I would be a journalist and that Deblauwe, having returned from Paris, would become my partner? And that one day Danse, finding himself in need of a magazine…

And that the Fakir would come to seek his fortune in Liège and would dazzle us with his experiences while Little K…

To get home, I passed by the church of Saint-Pholien every evening… I also passed by the hardware shop of Deblauwe's parents…

I was fifteen and a half years old and, without knowing it, without realising it, I was about to see three crimes interlocking around me.

While waiting, I was learning the words of '*La Madelon*' by heart, and patriotically collecting the tunic buttons of all the allied armies.

2

I can see again some people appearing suddenly, running around and shouting in a quiet street; I can see again a frantic woman trying in vain to escape from her pursuers, who literally swoop down on her. And then, for several minutes, there are vague movements, rumblings and gestures, which are incomprehensible at a distance, in an almost respectful silence, as at an execution, which is broken only by the wailings of the woman who no longer has the strength to struggle.

However, among so many clothed beings, one body appears completely naked, more crudely naked than anywhere else in the cold light of the street, on the hard grey of the cobblestones. The laughter freezes, and it is impossible to look away from the sharp dark triangle on the pale stomach...

Kids like me creep around, sick with emotion. A gossip, armed with scissors, cuts the woman's hair close to her skull, and she is forced to get up and walk along by the houses, while a hundred people form a procession behind her.

At that moment no one wondered if it was tragic or comic, nor what the reactions of the soldier would be, who, in two or three days, would find his wife again without her hair and would thus learn that she had given herself to the Germans.

Every week you could see seizures of arms and patriotic ceremonies taking place, and on all the farms the pigs were called Guillaume.[7]

Danse, gleaming and prosperous, a monstrous doll of 130 kilos in his new uniform, toured the little villages, and below his name as a comic singer, could be read: '*Former prisoner of the Germans*'.

Was it true? Was it false? No one really knew any more. And, from the moment that it was printed, that the authorities allowed it to be done... Besides the authorities knew nothing about it any more and had enough work to do organising processions to quench the thirst for heroism among the civilians.

Moreover, Danse, in his bookshop, did not remain inactive. In careful writing and on sumptuous velour he was writing some poems: 'Ode to Albert the First', 'Ode to Foch', 'Ode to Clemenceau'...[8]

Was he a great fool or very crafty? He never bothered about a publisher and did not try to reach out to the public. He was happy to make several copies of his odes, decorating them with arabesques, flags, drawings of flowers, lettering like that on manuscripts or for greetings on New Year's Day.

At that time, having some experience of these matters, he sent them, with a respectful letter, to the interested parties: the King, Foch, Clemenceau, and all the others, all those who had just gone down in history.

Below his signature he did not fail to mention that he was a 'civilian victim of the Barbarians'. So that, a few weeks later, he would receive some large official envelopes.

Sir,
His Majesty very much appreciated...

These letters from illustrious men were to decorate the display window of the second-hand bookseller, surrounded by ribbons in the national colours, and in 1933, a few days before his triple crime, he was to publish the list of all the testimonials of that kind that he had received, and which took up no less than one page of a newspaper.

In the meantime I became, at sixteen years old, his colleague, not yet as a journalist but in the bookselling business. The death of my father forced me to work, and, for a month, I was a sales assistant in a bookshop and reading room, the clients of which were my secondary school classmates, and from where I was to get myself dismissed for lack of respect towards the boss.

It was still the patriotic period. The women were wearing police-style hats and people talked about the 'Role of the Combatant', stripes, the trenches and decorations, when, one morning, for no reason, simply because I was passing in front of a newspaper office, I decided to go in and ask for a job as reporter.

I was sixteen years and a few months old. The following day I took up my duties and, from then on, I went up to Fort Loncin a hundred times a year, following all kinds of delegations: the Municipal Council of Paris, the American Mothers, Negus of Ethiopia or Prince Hirohito, the King of Italy, the chairman of the board of somewhere or other, unchanging ceremonies, a procession of cars from the station, which was decked out with flags, the endless road to the heroic fort and the speech by its commander, and then the return journey via the Herstal arms factory (a champagne toast), and the triumphant arrival at the Town Hall (a standing lunch), and then…

I belonged to the most respectable newspaper in the town and I was the youngest of the journalists. I still recall that, for the first official dinner that I attended, I borrowed not a dinner jacket, which I considered common, but a grey morning coat, and I am not sure if I didn't wear with it a white tie and gloves the colour of fresh butter.

Well, some time after that, during a grand lunch, which was, I think, given the title of a lunch for the Fervent City, I suddenly stood up at the table of honour, where I happened to be with my colleagues, and spoke out loudly and clearly: 'I'm clearing off! It's bloody boring!'

After which there was an immense void. When I woke up I was in my bed, with a heavy head thumping like a drum. A little later I found my mother sobbing and my brother looking at me in horror.

'What's happened?' I asked in a casual tone.

'Don't you know that some neighbours picked you up from the doorstep at six o'clock in the morning, and that three people were needed to carry you to your bed?'

No, I didn't know. And I examined with astonishment an enormous dagger, which had been found, it seemed, in the pocket of my gabardine.

'What have you done?'

How did I know? They could have declared that I had killed someone and I would have believed it.

The first thing I do is to dash off to the newspaper office, with the idea of telephoning my colleagues, to find out about my movements. In the hallway I am met by the caretaker who shakes his head in despair.

'My God! How could you do that...?'

'Do what?'

'You don't know? It's a disaster!'

And I learned that I had arrived at the newspaper office, without my hat, and with a broken walking stick in my hand, at about five o'clock in the afternoon, and that I vomited with all my might. The boss took care of me and tried to make me drink some hot coffee, in the usual way. But what is worse is that I hurled the coffee at his head, yelling, 'You're a great coward and you betrayed me! That's exactly what you are! I know what I'm saying!'

Now, he just waits for me, as is only right. He starts by firing me. Then he calls me back, because he is a nice man and informs me that he will give it a try again with me, but that I won't be sent to banquets any more.

At this point, a colleague rings me up.

'Are you better? Did you find your dancing girl?'

'My dancing girl?'

'It would be a good idea to drop by the Trianon to apologise...'

'Apologise for what?'

'Phone Deblauwe. He was the one who mixed the drinks in your glass. He didn't know that it would take effect so suddenly. He followed you around all afternoon...'

Deblauwe! Oh yes! I hardly knew him. He was older than me, thirty years old at least, and he wore fitted overcoats that dazzled me and juggled with a cane with a golden pommel as he walked. He was a handsome chap, with fine features, curled moustaches, and with slightly affected gestures. Not only was he older than me but he had been a journalist in Paris, and in Liège he wrote a daily piece signing himself Vinicius.

'Hallo! Deblauwe? Tell me, old chap, it seems that yesterday…'

Little by little the blanks in my memory were filled in like the squares on a lottery ticket and I found out about everything: that on leaving the banquet in the midst of a glacial silence, I dashed off to the Trianon theatre, where there was a matinee. I burst into the backstage area, set off in pursuit of a dancing girl and went across the stage after her yelling, and then…

'If I knew you were such a brat!…' Deblauwe said contemptuously.

To calm me down he took me to a brothel where he had some lady friends, and it was there, apparently, that I pinched the dagger, after having torn a dress or a blouse…

It doesn't matter… It's over… I was not fired from the newspaper, and I shall get off with having to put up with, to the end of my days, the reproaches of my mother, who was upset above all by the fact that I had been picked up by the neighbours.

What matters is that from now on I am Deblauwe's friend, and that, as our editorial offices are close to each other, we will be walking every day along the same way that separates us from our district, he handling his stick with a noble air and looking impertinently at the passers-by, while ceaselessly throwing out remarks, stating the obvious, and me, attentive and admiring, at least until the day when…

We shall meet each other again constantly on pilgrimages to Loncin, on visits by aristocratic foreigners to the arms factory, at ceremonies at the Town Hall, at reunions for war veterans, at musical parades and at patriotic or literary conferences.

On some occasions one of us will go on behalf of both of us and phone up his colleague the following morning.

'You understand?' Deblauwe says to me, 'In Paris we had things organised differently. I remember Clemenceau saying to me one day...'

'You know Clemenceau?'

'My God! We worked in the same office. A good chap, basically. I don't know how many times I dined with him in the rue du Croissant. I even said to Tardieu...'[9]

I don't want to brag, but I swear that in spite of everything I was already a little sceptical. And yet I did not yet have any connection with Hyacinthe Danse, who put up in his shop window letters from King Albert, Poincaré[10] and many important persons.

Many years later, after Danse had done his killings, Maurice Garçon would repeat often, in the course of his plea, the word paranoiac.

And in Paris, during about the same period as Deblauwe had also killed someone, I think that his lawyer did not fail to employ an identical argument.

'You understand! Here they know nothing about journalism, nor about anything, whatever it may be! They talk about the war without suspecting that we, in the Deuxième Bureau...'[11]

'Oh! You were...?'

'My God! Well now... I remember that one evening, while we were dining, Elisabeth confessed to me: "My dear Deblauwe, it's necessary to..."'

'Sorry! Which Elisabeth?'

'The Queen!'

I was sixteen-and-a-half or seventeen years old, do you understand? I listened. And I watched with a certain respect this man who drank those aperitifs with added water, while I contented myself with beer.

One day he really amazed me. He had taken me once again to that famous brothel, which I could not even remember anything about, as I was so drunk the first time.

He did not enter it furtively, hugging the walls, as I had always seen him do, but on the contrary he did it with a certain ostentation, and he would not have minded having himself photographed on the doorstep.

With his sombrero thrown back, his hands in his pockets, his walking stick resting on his shoulder like a sword, and a cigarette stuck on his lower lip, he pushed open the door of the 'mirror salon' and grumbled towards the manageress, 'How are things?'

'And you, Monsieur Ferdinand?'

'Is Renée upstairs? Get someone to serve us a drink. And do call someone to keep my friend company…'

Casually he went behind the scenes, and I could hear him making jokes in some room or other where the women were. Then he went upstairs, where Renée had not got up yet.

'You're a friend of Ferdinand's,' asked the woman wearing a shift, who came and sat down beside me on the seat covered with purple velvet. 'Is it true that he wants to take Renée to Spain?'

'I don't know…'

She did not need to observe me for long to realise that I did not know much.

'What do you want to drink?'

Deblauwe came down again, as if he were in his own home, opened a cupboard and poured himself a vermouth. Then, in a hushed voice, he talked with the madam and I realised that they were talking about money.

'If that's what she's told you, then she hasn't done anything more, my love. As you well know, Renée is straight up.'

Finally he sat down and the conversation turned to general matters. He talked about the newspaper and current events as a man who knew the inside stories, and the residents came one by one and sat down around him.

'Do you think they'll hang the Kaiser?'

For it was still one of the things that people were concerned about at that time.

'And the mark? My friend went over to Germany last week, where he bought a gold watch for 30 francs…'

Deblauwe was insensitive to so many naked thighs and to the breasts that sometimes slipped out of blouses.

I saw Renée come down. She was quite a stout woman, dark-haired and a little hairy with a slightly husky voice. She immediately ordered a drink.

An hour later, in the street, he explained to me, not without pride: 'What if I told you she brings me in more than I earn at the newspaper? That's the reason why I'd like to set her up in Barcelona. Over there things are much better than here.'

A month later he announced to me calmly, 'Come and see my printing works…'

It was not a bluff. He had set up a printing works and owned machines, workers, proofreaders, all without giving up his duties at the newspaper.

'Write me a novel and I'll publish it for you!'

Nor was this a bluff either. He published two or three novels by young authors, and the appearance of his books filled us with wonder because of their modernity.

However he also published a political review in collaboration with a foreigner, and, one fine day, he declared to us, 'They're forcing me to close down.'

'Who?'

'The Deuxième Bureau.'

This time I think it was true, for much later I found the name of Deblauwe's collaborator on the list of suspicious people of most western countries.

Danse and Deblauwe did not yet know each other. Or rather Danse must have read some time the articles signed Vinicius while Deblauwe, like everybody else, would have glanced at the second-hand bookseller's dubious window display.

Well, if the two of them were destined to kill, a few months apart, they were also, within an interval of a few weeks, to perform a similar deed.

Both of them came from good families. The one had studied with the Jesuits, and the other had done so at a secondary school.

Each of them has a mother who is a good woman, belonging to that class of petit bourgeois, whose honesty is almost Jansenist.[12]

During the war Danse frequents the Kommandantur.

After the war, Deblauwe sets up a printing works with money from a foreign government.

Danse collects patiently the testimonials of important people and writes poems that are corny by dint of their conformism.

At the same time Deblauwe creates doggerel every day in his newspaper, signed with the name Vinicius, and, in private, talks only of his relationships with the powerful people of the day.

Deblauwe was formerly married and is divorced. In his turn, Danse also gets a divorce.

During the war, Danse made use of his mysterious passport to attract young girls to his house.

Deblauwe rents a small pied-à-terre not far from the Girls Middle School, looks out for the pupils at the exit and attracts them with the prospect of gaudy aperitifs and pastries.

This does not prevent Deblauwe from setting off one fine morning for Barcelona in the company of Renée and setting her up in a house over there where she will bring him in two or three times as much as in the past.

Round about the same time, Hyacinthe Danse goes on a trip to the South of France and, while he set off alone, he returns in the company of a woman.

It's not Renée. That would be too much to hope for. That would be like in a novel. But it is someone like her, a keeper in a brothel, whom Danse sets up in Liège and whom he goes to see just as the other man goes to see his mistress.

With the one as with the other, is there any love involved?

I won't take responsibility for answering this. Danse, in any case, will kill his mistress on the day when she decides to leave him. And when Deblauwe bumps off Tejalda with several revolver shots, in a furnished flat in the rue de Maubeuge, it will be because the Spaniard has taken his 'woman'.

At that time I knew nothing of this yet. Nobody knew, not even those concerned. Three times a week I went to look for books in Danse's shop and discussed with him the new publications, or also I would spend hours trying craftily to buy an original edition off him at a low price.

He was fiendishly good at playing to the gallery and I would bet that he studied his facial expressions in front of a mirror. On the other hand, there was one disturbing detail that I had noticed, because I was at an age when such things do not escape you. For living amongst his dusty books, he had adopted a white apron. Now, beneath the apron, his hand was always in his pocket and I found there was a dubious moistness about his smile.

They continued to go up to Fort Loncin and to put the regiments on parade, and the war veterans organised processions while the police started, here and there, to arrest communist agents, about which we knew next to nothing.

My first novel had just been written when Deblauwe's printing works closed its doors. It was entitled *On the Bridge of Arches*, the bridge the two of us crossed every day chatting together.

I had learned not to cause a scandal at the banquets any more and not to throw hot coffee at the head of my editor-in-chief, so much so that my newspaper, reassured despite its strictness, did not get worried about the company I kept.

One evening, instead of taking me to the usual knocking shop, where he no longer had any commercial interests, Deblauwe took me to L'Ane Rouge,[13] and I discovered there a universe that was completely unfamiliar to me.

It was in a squalid street wedged between two big main roads, and was a Montmartre-style cabaret, with death's heads on the walls, caricatures of great men and of cabaret artists, imitation rustic furniture, with a few performers from Paris who earned twenty francs a day and who stayed in the house.

One of them who stayed there a long time has become almost famous. A young girl, who sang songs full of realism in a husky voice, enjoyed sudden fame in the music halls of Paris and died the year after.

Deblauwe fitted in with as much ease as he did in the brothel and he introduced me to a bunch of noisy customers, and it was they who struck up in unison with '*Les Moines de Saint Bernadin*'...[14]

'My friends the painters...'

Among them was Little K... And near the bar was a person with long, greasy hair, and a grimy collar, who was constantly stuffing something up his nose, and who looked at us without seeing us. We did not interest him. He was watching the real clients, those who were getting plastered and who had money in their pockets. He went up to their table, gloomily and full of scorn.

'Would you like me to tell you how you will die?... Give me your hand... Give it to me!'

He would take it by force if need be, then sit down, drink from the client's glass and groan, 'I see a serious accident... You have never been strong...'

I did not know yet who he was. I did not know anyone, and, as I had learned '*La Madelon*' after the war, I tried to remember the refrains of the drinking songs, above all those in Latin, which I found particularly charming.

'Will you have a glass?' said Deblauwe when the Fakir had finished with a nouveau riche. 'Is the *business* going well?'

'The stingy sods! The c...!'

'May I introduce...'

The room was small, filled with smoke, and was a kind of imitation of Le Lapin Agile.[15] Cabaret artists and women who were reciters came to sit at our table after their turn at singing and they charged us 'performers' prices'.

Apart from my historic binge, I was not used to drinking, and at about three o'clock in the morning, while I was returning home with a friend, I would have been hard put to provide any details about the evening.

What I do know is that I stopped in the middle of the bridge and looked at the River Meuse swathed in fog and declaimed haughtily, 'At forty I'll be a minister or a member of the Académie Française.'

For, from then on, I had as friends people who all seemed to me to have been destined for the highest places, from the Fakir, who claimed to be an authentic Hindu fakir, to those young painters who talked about Rembrandt as if he were a colleague, with K... also among them, and each one of them told me repeatedly that he had as much genius as Verlaine.[16]

Consequently, why couldn't I also have some kind of genius? I did not yet know exactly what kind. Perhaps for politics? Perhaps for literature?

I slept too heavily. The next day, my mother looked at me suspiciously and felt the need to remind me of the business with the dagger.

'At your age, your father would not have been allowed to come home at three o'clock in the morning...'

From then on I would be coming home very much later, at four, at five o'clock and even not at all, simply because Deblauwe had made me acquainted with the Fakir, the bunch of painters, Little K... and that...

And that all this, to say it one more time, would end up with deaths, people in prison or in the penal colony, with...

The period of war was over, with its young girls under gas lamps and on the wet doorsteps; the period of patriotism was over, with its pilgrimages to Loncin and visits by foreign diplomats to the National Arms Factory; another period was beginning, artistic, mystical, frenzied and chaotic, and it was this that would lead to the first death.

Now, in this same period, Danse developed a passion for occult sciences, and, if it was difficult for him to claim the title of Fakir, he was to lose no time in granting himself that of Magus.

Only to finish also in blood!

3

'Oh! The voluptuousness of clasping a virgin with a pus-filled navel!' exclaimed this twenty-year-old painter, with a gloomy look in his eyes.

I have to relate in detail how things happened in this new world into which Deblauwe had introduced me, one evening at L'Ane Rouge, while the Fakir was earning his living interpreting the lines in people's palms with an air of supreme disgust.

There were a few – or rather there were a few of us, since I was to become one of them for a short time – who frequented in rather desultory fashion the Academy of Fine Arts and wore the romantic garb of poor painters, a black sombrero and floppy bow tie.

They came from all districts of the town and from all classes of society: one was the son of a big manufacturer of shoe polish, and the father of another, Little K..., was a poor unskilled worker, who was a widower and always drunk; there were sons of shopkeepers and one of a university professor; the youngest were eighteen years old, and the eldest twenty-three or twenty-four.

Did their mysticism, which I would adopt at the same time as the floppy bow tie, come from the war or quite simply from the accursed poets whom they heard reciting at L'Ane Rouge? Was it born of a book that had been poorly read and poorly digested by one of them?

I don't know anything about it. It's especially nowadays that I ask myself about it. For, at the end of the day, while at college I had taken part in the football team and my greatest pleasure, since I had been a reporter, was to get away on a motorbike to the countryside.

I read a lot, admittedly, but the authors I preferred were Balzac, Dickens and Dumas, who have nothing particularly morbid about them. And I am sure that, if at that time there had existed gangs of young people and groups of girls who went dashing off every Saturday to the exuberant world of nature, armed with skis, or fold-up dinghies, with camping tents or equipment for physical exercise, I would have joined them enthusiastically.

But there weren't any! A town like Liège had only a few painting exhibitions every week, which the entire population marched off to, and the newspapers, which did not yet have three pages of sports, devoted columns to twenty-year-old daubers and booklets of verse.

So the heroes of the day were my new friends, who could stride around Le Carré in certain knowledge that everyone was looking at them.

Just as at L'Ane Rouge I had had to learn '*Les Moines de Saint Bernardin*', and as at the armistice I had discovered '*La Madelon*', I now, renouncing Balzac and Dumas, had to discuss endlessly 'the infinite' and 'the indefinite', 'the objective' and 'the subjective', the supremacy of Rembrandt or of Leonardo da Vinci, of Baudelaire or of Verlaine, of Plato or of Pyrrhon...

Are there still young people existing somewhere nowadays, who wildly pursue stimulation, as we used to then, stimulation of anything, of the body, of the senses, of the mind, by all imaginable means and even by tricks, and according to meticulously codified formulae resembling those of sexual maniacs?

At the start it was nothing more than a chance, impromptu affair. We got together randomly, sometimes at one person's house, sometimes at another's, and most often at the home of a painter, who had a studio in his parents' loft. In his pocket each one of us brought a bottle and the latest poem he had dug up, or some bright philosophical idea.

It could not go on like that. The unfortunate person at whose home it took place had to stand up the following day to his indignant family, who had not been able to close their eyes all night and who found piles of vomit everywhere, on the staircase and in the toilets, broken objects and the telephone torn out, if not two or three deathly pale young people left on the landings...

Besides, with regard to stimulation, we became more and more difficult to please. We needed numerous accessories, and so it was that one fine day the '*caque*'[17] was born.

Behind the church of Saint-Pholien, in a ruined house, at the back of a courtyard of modest craftsmen, there was a room that had formerly served as a cabinetmaker's studio, which we rented for the modest sum of thirty or forty francs a month. The decor was as medieval as you could wish, and the entrance to it was so sinister that none of us would dare to venture there alone.

However, the first object that we took there was a skeleton that was almost complete and a piece of cheap red cotton material. As for me, I brought a cheap chandelier discovered in my mother's loft, the disappearance of which she has never been able to understand.

What else was there? Everything and nothing. Mysterious inscriptions drawn from *Le Grand Albert*[18] and drawings of erotic nudes on the walls, chipped cups, glasses that had never been washed and, finally, increasingly numerous empty bottles.

In the evening, when dinner was finished, each of us would leave his parents' house and soon some of us were at the *caque*, delving into the bottoms of our pockets for money to buy drink, of any kind, a drink that for the least money would make you drunk the quickest.

My chandelier provided far too much light and instead we preferred a candle, surrounded in addition by so much red paper that you could not see anything any more and could only make out the shapes stretched out on the floor or on the mattresses, and the faces made deathly pale by the reddish light, all of which however were the faces of seventeen- to twenty-year-olds.

The *Dies Irae* was almost always a prelude to the evening, unless it was *De Profundis*, and finally, from the shadows, someone would throw in a remark: 'If Rembrandt were to come back again in our time…'

'Who mentioned Rembrandt? I say that still life painting…'

The Meuse flowed close by. Somewhere people must have been living a normal life, while at the back of a squalid yard discussion was warming up, and we hurled quotations in each other's faces from Greek or Latin philosophers, whom we had discovered that very day, and finally decided to make peace with each other, in tearful embraces.

For we were constantly going off in search of more bottles, in the last cafés that had stayed open. A new arrival found himself surrounded by anxious faces.

'How much have you got on you?'

'Six francs...'

'Give it to us! There's nothing more to drink.'

We smoked a lot. The atmosphere became thick with it. Someone sobbed for no reason, without anyone worrying about it, and another, always the same person, would suddenly get undressed and wrap himself in an old scarlet dressing gown and exclaim, in a tragic, inspired voice, 'If God the Father suddenly came in, what do you think he would say when he saw me? Well, I'm asking him, I ask God the Father to have the courage to push this door open and reveal himself...'

No one laughed. It was late. The town was asleep and tense faces turned towards that door that might perhaps move.

'God the Father, listen to me! Don't think that I'm joking! I am sincere! I ask you once... twice... three times...'

And someone murmured with a shudder, 'What about summoning up the devil?'

'Which one?'

Then, suddenly, Little K..., who was draining everyone's glasses, rolled on the floor, dribbling and groaning, racked by a nervous attack or an epileptic fit.

'Satan,' a voice yelled out, 'is it you who manifests yourself through the medium of our friend K...? If it is, reply...'

Wine worked out too expensive and took too long to produce the desired effect. Even spirits soon seemed too slow to us and one of us, whose girlfriend was a sales assistant in a chemist's, brought a bottle of ether one evening.

He also brought his girlfriend, whose name was Charlotte, and who found somewhere to sit on one of the couches among the sagging bodies.

'... clasping a virgin with a pus-filled navel...'

The person, who proclaimed this desire, without laughing, was a young twenty-year-old painter, handsome and illustrious, and known all over town through his exhibitions, at which he sold everything he wanted to.

He was also the one who, at two o'clock in the morning, challenged God the Father, and who, one hour later, flung himself down on his knees and demanded to make his confession to everyone, so that he would be punished for his pride.

Deblauwe came sometimes, stayed for a few minutes, uttered only some contemptuous words, and threw an inquisitive glance at Charlotte or at another young girl who was there.

A young sixteen-year-old dancer who was phthisical and diaphanous, never missed a single meeting and trembled for hours on end, with frantic eyes, with rings round them, and staring into space...

'Whoever doesn't believe in genius, or in God...'

But weren't we all geniuses? Geniuses who, unfortunately, did not have very strong stomachs, nor nerves, so much so that at first light pathetic scenes occurred.

There were other scenes, no less stormy, in the following days with the parents, who saw their kids coming home at dawn with red eyelids, with furry mouths and disdainful expressions.

One of our friends worked at a photographer's, where he made pantograph enlargements in charcoal, which did not prevent him from painting after a day's work and spending the greater part of his nights at the *caque*.

K..., the poorest of all, got himself taken on two or three times a week at some building site or other, lugging bricks, chucking mortar or climbing ladders.

One evening, when the door opened, we could make out in the semi-darkness a long yellow face and greasy hair that hung down in rolls on the velvet collar of a cape: it was the Fakir, who had been invited and who had deigned to cede to our entreaties.

That lasted several hours. On the table near the candle there was a sheet of paper fixed by four drawing pins. This sheet was covered with lines close together, and between two of these lines a matchstick had been placed. Now, without any other accessories, we were going to manage to make ourselves so nervously ill that our hearts beat too fast, and we became so short of breath that it induced hysterical cries and drained us of energy more effectively than the worst of orgies.

There were six, or were there perhaps eight of us?

'There's still too much light,' said the Fakir in that voice of his, which was as oily as his skin and his Levantine-style hair. He was a head taller than us and all the time he shook the flaps of his cape, to take out a little bit of white powder from one of his pockets.

The candle was placed at the other end of the room, so that we had to make a constant effort to make out the pencil lines around the matchstick.

'Focus your entire will in looking at this matchstick. Everyone touch the hand of both his neighbours. You will see the bit of wood move, change its position to another box... Be careful! Don't move any more...'

The pencil lines ended up dancing about on your retina and today I am unable to say if that match moved. Besides, after several hours, as our nerves were exposed, a discussion took place that finished by degenerating into a fight, because two factions formed on the question of the Fakir and his power.

'Very well then! Since you doubt me, I'm going to put one of you into a cataleptic fit...'

He chose Little K... who recoiled involuntarily. Did he get what he was looking for? I certainly don't think so, but in the early morning our friend was bloodless and his lips were still trembling.

'Tomorrow... In a few days... I have to get used to the medium...'

None of us at that time seemed to have any idea of going swimming in the rivers and frolicking about on the grass! Not even one of us thought of simple amorous adventures.

There were a few girls, Charlotte, stupid and placid, the chemist's little salesgirl, who would not live long, and one or two others as well, and they were enough for all of us.

' ...a virgin who would have a navel...'

We used to say to Charlotte, 'You're ugly and stupid! You smell bad. I despise you, but I need to make love and you will disgust me even more after...'

And Charlotte accepted it, because in a confused way she saw her existence as being involved with that of the new Rembrandts and the new Villons.

With a glum indifference, she gave everyone the same bugs and the same disease, which fortunately was not serious.

Weren't we, at that time, quite close to Hyacinthe Danse, who was devouring *Le Grand Albert* and all those books on magic, in the back of his shop, and who would later go and find his mistress at home. With the one difference perhaps: that our sincerity was absolute!

Alas, while some of us, after leaving the *caque*, found a well-served table, fairly good hygiene and a soothing atmosphere at their homes, others, the poorest ones, found only a dirty little bedsitter, a drunken father, or loneliness and irregular meals.

The Fakir had promised to show us K... in a cataleptic fit and he kept his word a few days later. He had made the most of this delay and lived with K... in the hotel where he was staying, a fantastic hotel, frequented only by circus and music-hall freaks.

When they came back to the *caque* together, K... was more colourless than ever and followed the other man like an automaton.

'I order you to sleep!'

It did not take long. After a few spasms the kid was as rigid as a log, and, poised between two chairs, with his head and feet barely touching the edges of each of them, he supported the weight of three of us without giving way.

'K..., tell us what you see... I want you to go in search of your mother... Can you find her?...'

We trembled. Our throats were dry. We all knew that K...'s mum had died destitute and that for him it was an agonising memory.

So, to hear him say, with indifference, in a changed voice, 'I can see her... But she doesn't seem to recognise me...'

'What is she doing?'

'I don't know... She's holding a small piece of paper in her hand... She's talking to someone... Wait...!'

And suddenly the crisis occurred and K..., who struggled, yelled, dribbled and finally opened his eyes, stayed for a long time without recognising us and finally smiled a shy smile.

'What happened?'

What it took us several days to discover, was that the Fakir was dosing him up with cocaine and that K... was at his heels all day and all night.

What savour could there be from then on to our philosophical discussions and to the addresses to God the Father, who never deigned to appear? We had K... We had the Fakir. We were so proud of them that one day we invited the students to be present at the experiments.

It was Christmas Eve. The stocks of liquid were on that account more abundant than usual and the students, for their part, had brought some too. In a room capable of holding twenty people there were perhaps fifty of us, who were soon drunk, some sick, others declaiming, yelling or moaning, and jostling each other around one of our friends, who out of vanity sported a dinner jacket with a shirt front that stuck out provocatively.

'Today the Arts welcome Science...'

And there were moist kisses, bottles broken at the neck against the table, and voices asking, 'Where d'you piss here?'

'Anywhere, my old friend!... In the skull. Here you are!... Or against the wall...'

And we did it, while once again the Fakir tried out his power over K..., who soon fell into a cataleptic fit.

I don't know what visions he had that night, nor what words he uttered in that 'disembodied' voice that he adopted then. There were too many people. Someone grabbed you by the shoulders and swore to you that it was the most beautiful night of his life, and another begged you to give him a glass of water. You heard people talking about Dante and Shakespeare, and still about Plato and Rembrandt, while some students, who were really somewhat behind us, were still repeating in unison '*Les Moines de Saint Bernardin*'.

I would like to be able to say now that Danse was there. But he was not. There were only us, K...'s friends, the Fakir and the students, who played the role of extras.

In Liège tradition requires that on Christmas Eve you should be present at the performance by the Puppet Theatre, which takes place in an alleyway of the most populous outer suburbs. Everybody went. It rained. You went in batches into a narrow room where the theatre was and where you were crushed together against other night owls, while the voice of the compère, thick with wine, told the story of the nativity in his own way.

Then we looked for each other in the alleyways, tripped over the pavements and went sprawling in the puddles of water.

'Who's going to carry him? He's really ill...'

K... was stretched out stiff on the ground, as I had been on the evening when I first got plastered. They hoisted him onto my shoulder. He had lost a shoe, one of his socks was wet and his feet were dirty; his body was too light and someone behind me held up his head.

'Where does he live?'

And all of a sudden we realised that none of us knew where K... lived! He was our friend. He spent all his time with us, but we knew nothing of his ordinary life.

'His father lives in the suburbs. But he must have a room somewhere...'

Someone gave an address, which was not right, and we needlessly made some nice people, who were sleeping, get up. Then we went somewhere else, with K... still on my shoulder, in the rain, with whiffs of wine and song.

'I think it's here...'

It was nearby, but we searched K...'s pockets in vain to find a key. They contained only a dirty handkerchief, two stubs of pencil and small change.

A fat woman in a camisole received us at the top of some stairs.

'It's not worth bringing him back...'

'Why?'

'Because I don't want him here any more in any case. In the first place, how come he goes eight days without coming back?'

How was I to know? He must have slept at the Fakir's home.

'Oh well! Put him in his room anyway. But not in the bed: he'd make it all dirty...'

There was no electricity. I lit an oil lamp and saw on an easel a strange picture sketched out, with a livid sky, the spire of a church, a deserted place...

'Don't you think it's better to call a doctor?'

'He's asleep... He's even starting to snore...'

I did not know where the Fakir had gone to. We could only find here and there some remaining members of the group and there was no more to drink. We wandered around the streets, on principle, occasionally trying a refrain, which we did not feel like singing.

Several of our companions of that night must have become doctors, lawyers or magistrates.

In my case, arriving at my newspaper office the following day, I found among the police reports that were passed on to us every morning:

> In the early hours the body of a young twenty-year-old man, of no occupation, by the name of K..., was discovered hanging in the doorway of the church of Saint-Pholien...

A little later, we were to meet again at the central police station with Deblauwe, who, like me, did the stories about dogs that had got run over.

'You're idiots!' he said to me that day, shrugging his shoulders. 'You'll see! Some day or other you'll get yourselves in damned trouble.'

At what time had K... woken up? And what could he have been thinking, in the state in which he found himself? He had a shoe missing. His socks were wet. Perhaps he had not taken a bath in weeks.

No one, not even his landlady, had heard him sneak out like a rat, and no one had seen him in the streets, when probably it had not yet become light.

The church was only a hundred metres from the *caque*... The Fakir must have been sleeping in his hotel stuffed with circus freaks...

One of the first persons that I saw again was Charlotte, whom one mainly came across in the evening and could then take to the *caque*, for which she had a key, in anticipation of providing precisely those sorts of favours.

'Is it true, what they're saying about K...?'

'It's true.'

'The poor chap!'

I tried to find out if he too had resorted to the good services of Charlotte, but she shook her head.

'Never! And I think he never touched another girl either. He wasn't interested in such things...!'

My God! He came from further away than all of us, from a dump of a sordid suburb where a drunkard beat his mother, and from where she then left, half-dead, one fine morning for the hospital and the cemetery.

Who had given him the idea of painting? By what miracle had he met us? And why had he believed, with all his might, and full of rage...?

What he believed in I have no idea. In everything we said – and we said so many things! Believed in our stories about genius and demons, about Plato and Verlaine, about God the Father and hypnotism...

As for us, I plead not guilty, do you see? Or rather I plead non-premeditation and even ignorance. We did not know! It could have happened to us too, as it happened to Danse who, at that time, was already a man, and to Deblauwe, who had more experience than us.

But there was one of them who knew what he was doing, a man who came into the *caque* one evening, looking mysterious and cynical in his cape with a velvet collar and who looked at us one after the other with eyes capable of weighing us up morally.

He understood well at first glance, that it was K... whom he should choose. And he understood, from experience, how to break down a poor boy in bad health.

He forgot nothing, neither his mother whom it was necessary to invoke, nor the cocaine, which is more crucial, in this case, than the alcohol and even our ether.

Two or three times he had K... come to L'Ane Rouge and the public had been very impressed. Perhaps, if the kid had been a little stronger he would have provided a good music-hall or cabaret act for several months...

We saw the Fakir again, hugging the walls, turning back, when he caught sight of one of us from afar.

At the *caque*, a few days after that, someone suddenly got up, with eyes bulging: 'Who brought the ether here?... Let him speak!... Otherwise he will be excluded...'

For the result was that ether now seemed to be something criminal to us, and a poor chap who had taken to it seriously was excluded, indeed rejected by *the number of human beings to whom it is permitted to speak*.

At about the same time, a nineteen-year-old designer who had met, at L'Ane Rouge, a fifty-year-old 'diva', confided in us, sobbing, 'You don't know what it's like old friend!... You can't know what it's like!... I was sleeping... And all of a sudden, when I wake up, I see her sitting near the window, busy darning my socks... Imagine if, after that, it is for the rest of your life!... Darning my socks!... She!... A woman!...'

It's true that the boy had never, so to speak, known his mother.

And another, who had never despised the dull embraces of Charlotte, made a long speech to us one evening on Greek sculpture.

'Have you ever seen a work by Phidias covered with ridiculous hair? No, right? So, therefore, why don't we also remove all our hair, in the name of beauty?'

'You've done it, have you?'

'A little while ago in the bath...'

But a few hours later when he was drunk he confessed, 'I'm a liar, a rotten liar! It's not because of Greek statues... It's because of that filthy trash Charlotte, who has given us all the...'

The reason for telling about this is so that you don't forget that we were between seventeen and twenty-four years old.

Danse, shut up in the back of his shop, also engaged in magic, but *in a different way*.

And Deblauwe, always sure of himself, presented himself at my house one morning, while I was shaving, though whether my chin had any great need of it...? It wasn't to talk about K..., or about the Fakir, Rembrandt or Plato.

'Get dressed quickly! Come with me! Today we can both make our fortune!

And my mother, who had not heard however, was not all that reassured by this untimely visit.

4

A few weeks ago, far from Liège and our youth, the police in Nantes were notified by an anonymous letter that some strange events were taking place in a cellar. The newspapers only said a few words about it, and I suppose that serious-minded people shrugged their shoulders and talked of it as childishness. As for me, there was not a single detail that I did not devour greedily.

First of all the name of the street, rue de la Fosse, which reminded me of our Cour des Miracles[19] behind the church of Saint-Pholien.

And then the sight that must have amazed the police so much and which would not have surprised me at all: as the investigating officers burst into the room, they caught sight of three young people standing there, with their heads concealed in hoods, lit up by church candles and by seven-branched candelabra decorated with candles.

So it was that, twenty years after us, adolescents were still getting themselves drunk on mystery, even if it was a crudely artificial mystery acquired by relying heavily on bad lighting and dressing up.

Did they also discuss Dante and Schopenhauer, Vishnu and Christ, whom we called more familiarly just Jesus.

At any rate they had started like us by installing a sort of couch against the wall. Also just like us, they had felt the need to blend a touch of eroticism with the decor and a death's head provided the essential macabre note.

'On this day, we, the undersigned, descendants of Adam and Eve, have founded, after a number of difficulties, the Clan of the Anonymous Ones.'

There was one difference to us, however: the members must have been fifteen to eighteen years old. So they were three or four years younger than us.

What do they intend to do? Are they going to sing '*Les Moines de Saint Bernardin*' in their cellar, or will they ask some fakir to put them in a trance?

They are, as we mostly were at that time, pupils at a Fine Arts school. And I wait impatiently to find out what they have achieved, what they dream of.

Someone has sent me some information about it. Taking their inspiration from a cartoon comic book called *Les Pieds-Nickelés chez les gangsters*,[20] they have been scouting the town for several months, emptying the collection boxes of churches with the aid of glue, and pinching from window displays.

This happened, I repeat, scarcely three months ago. Of course, the grown-ups did not understand and it all ended in more or less severe sermons.

But it was only a few days later when three members of the *Clan of the Anonymous Ones* doped themselves well on drinks, broke into a jeweller's and attacked the shopkeeper and her husband. And the person who inspired the crime was none other than the jeweller's son.

But then didn't we, at the *caque*, kill Little K… ?

I know that that morning, when Deblauwe was speaking to me about our fortune, was in the spring, and that the sun was completely fresh. I know it just as I know that it was rainy on Christmas night. I know it because that morning I shaved and chose a coloured tie.

Now, such details of dress were of major importance in that period. So, for weeks, the one amongst us who had the most influence on the others would wear a sombrero that was sort of grimy and a big floppy necktie on a rather dirty shirt.

So, it was a mystical period! At that time we hardly washed. Beards were growing, our hair became dishevelled and we savoured our own dirtiness. We declaimed from the works of Saint Francis of Assisi. We addressed 'my sister the moon, and my brother the horse', and if only our beards had been long enough, we would have been able to breed parasites in them, following the example of the great saint, in order to live in more perfect intimacy with the creatures of the Good Lord.

They were also times of drinking sessions and elation, of dizzy lyricism.

Then suddenly, one morning, because a slanting ray of sunlight came to tickle us in our beds, because there was a sense of spring in the air, one of us felt the need to clean himself up.

That morning Deblauwe watched me do it. The day before, I would not even have listened to him, because the day before I was writing some poetry about solitude:

'*Oh melancholy high church tower…*'

... The high church tower that is all alone and envies the humble houses cramped one against the other at its feet...

Now, Deblauwe came to talk to me about business, and I listened, because I had just shaved, filed my nails and was waiting there in boxer shorts for a crease to be put in my trousers, which had not had one for a long time.

'Do you understand? We're going to see him together. He'll supply the funds. And we'll edit the magazine together.'

God! On such mornings I renounced Dante, Schopenhauer and even Rembrandt and Shakespeare, and I renounced the *caque* and all the fakirs of the Orient. I needed to be as neat and clean as a cloudless sky, and I walked with a more elastic step, looking at myself with satisfaction in the glass panes of the shop windows.

It was the same with all our friends. Whenever, during a crisis of cleanliness, we met one who had not yet fallen into step and who talked to us about the church of Saint-Pholien, we looked at him in some embarrassment.

'... Yes... One of these days...'

So for several days, one or two pathetic individuals who were not up to date haunted the place with death's heads and candles.

At first sight this duality seems amusing. Still now I smile at it, but as soon as I think about it, I realise that it is all a drama that we bear within us, the eternal story of Dr Jekyll and Mr Hyde.

So Little K... died because he did not have the time to wash.

So some of us never had the time for it and stayed all their lives in the period of beards and drunken declamations.

Others have continued to alternate between the two states... Like Deblauwe, who killed someone one day when he was wearing an old gabardine bought for twenty francs at a flea market, and who had not worn a beard for several weeks...

Like Hyacinthe Danse, who has recently been devoting all his time to magic, his body greasy and unkempt and wrapped in a grimy dressing gown.

The streets themselves seemed to have had a wash, and Deblauwe and I went into a spacious district, with one- or two-storeyed houses, and windows decorated with green plants and embroidered curtains.

Here and there a woman was sluicing her bit of pavement and soaping the cut-stone doorstep with a brush. An official went from door to door, in order to remind those who had not already done it that they had to pull up the weeds growing between the cobblestones. For again and again throughout my childhood I pulled up weeds in the part of the road in front of our house, and I can remember the scratching sound of the knife against the stone...

There was no place so calm and orderly as that district, with sullen vendors going from door to door, one pushing a vegetable cart, another a coal cart, the milkman announcing his presence through a special trumpet and the baked-pear seller with his traditional cry.

It has to be said that for weeks, shut up in our *caque* and in our over-proud daydreams, we did not see any of all that, neither the buds that were bursting open on the trees in the small public garden, nor the beautiful girls in their bright aprons, in red and blue slippers, who ran, holding the buns in their hair, to the local butcher's.

Deblauwe rang at the door of an exceptionally comfortable-looking house that I knew well, because it had a special reputation. It was kept by two sisters, two quite beautiful women, one especially, who had thick brown hair, fine white flesh, and whom one could always catch a glimpse of dressed in an open dressing gown over her soft breasts.

My mother used to say:

'It's a "bad house"...'

It was a bad house because they let out furnished rooms there to rich students. Admittedly, in the whole district they let out rooms to students, but there were two categories of houses: those in which the tenants could not receive women and those to which there was, as we used to say, 'free access'.

Now, at the place where we rang the bell access was free, very free, and you could see lights on in the windows until late into the night with music seeping out beneath the doors.

They ushered us into a spacious apartment that smelt of eau de Cologne, and with my first glance, I was gaining a foothold in a new world.

First there was that woman in a silk dressing gown who guided us and who, with every step, let us glimpse her legs well up above her stockings...

She was wearing perfume, and, as she smoked, her lips left a red half-moon mark on the cigarette...

'Sit down... I'll tell him that you're here...'

It was not so much any detail as the atmosphere that excited me. The room, for example, was not furnished according to traditions that were current in my home or the homes of my friends. The furniture was in light lacquer, and on the unmade bed was an eiderdown in light pink. Nearby, on a pedestal table, there was still a tray with the remains of breakfast.

A voice came from the half-open bathroom, a man's voice, which said with a strong oriental accent, 'Is that you, Monsieur Deblauwe?... One minute... Take one of the cigarettes on the table...'

And we could hear some sounds of water.

'Bring me my dressing gown, Lola!' the voice went on. Quite naturally the woman went into the bathroom and I saw her, from the back, looking towards the bathtub where there was a naked man...

As for Deblauwe, he winked at me, and took one of the cigarettes on the table, cigarettes that were a great luxury, the brand name of which I didn't even know.

'There we are... I'm sorry, but I went to bed quite late...'

I thought he was magnificent! And magnificently affluent and unpretentious! He was still wet and his black hair was slightly curled. With no sense of modesty, nor the lack of it, he came towards us, drying his hairy chest under his floral dressing gown.

'How do you do?... Sit down... Lola! Bring us something to drink...'

He was a Romanian, thirty-five or forty years old, a handsome chap, a little fat, and he lisped and was, in my view, sumptuous. With the morning untidiness of his room, his semi-nudity, the negligee of the woman who was helping him, he seemed to me to fulfil the most Byzantine dreams and he embodied in my eyes the very model of the great lord.

The word mogul seemed to me to be suitable for him... On one finger he had an enormous ring, with a yellow diamond...

'Would you excuse me?'

There were maybe fifteen letters on a tray, and he cast a casual glance over them, while lighting his first cigarette with a gold lighter.

'Nothing interesting. What'll you have?... A glass of champagne?... vermouth?...'

He was not bluffing. A bottle of champagne was waiting in an ice bucket and our Romanian explained:

'In the morning I need it to clean my mouth... So, Monsieur Deblauwe?...'

I imagined that life in a palace must proceed like this, in voluptuous abandonment and in elegant disorder, and I admired it all confidently, including the sandals in red kid leather of our host.

'My friend and I,' Deblauwe then said, 'are prepared to take over the editorship of the magazine, as you suggested...'

I was not quite seventeen and a half years old, and in my periods of elegance and anti-mysticism I used to wear a false collar with broken tips and celluloid cuffs; moreover I considered it essential to decorate my varnished shoes with mouse-grey gaiters.

It was all or nothing! A few weeks earlier, I had my head shorn, to escape more certainly from the demon of vanity. Now, with a lot of help from cosmetics, I managed after a fashion to part my hair, which was too short, and, while listening to our Romanian, I resolved to perfume myself like him with Russian eau de Cologne and to sport one day a yellow diamond in a platinum signet ring.

'Have you thought of a title for your magazine?'

Of course it was to be a satirical magazine, in which we were going to chastise the people of Liège in a fine way. I was a humorist. There was no shadow of doubt about it, especially since my newspaper had entrusted me with the job of writing a daily piece. No absurdity escaped me, except my own collar with broken tips, my false shirt front with tie and my grey gaiters.

'*The Whip*,' I suggested timidly.

'I think that's already been used,' Deblauwe objected, who anyway had a little more experience than me.

'*The Riding Crop* then?'

Our Romanian friend liked the idea of the riding crop, as he was a man who liked to go for a ride on a horse along the streets.

'It would be better to use a local word,' recommended Deblauwe.

'*La Légia*? *The Fervent City*? *The Worthy Liège Citizen*?'[21]

In the meantime we drank champagne and Lola, who sat on the edge of the bed listening to us, had crossed her legs, which revealed below her suspenders an area of skin about ten centimetres square.

Just imagine, the Romanian lived with such sights before his eyes all day!

'Why not *Nanesse*?'

She is a person from Liège mythology, a coarse gossip, generally depicted with an avenging broom in her hand.

Having chosen the title, Deblauwe took numerous documents out of his briefcase, cited figures, the weight and price of paper, the cost of typesetting, rough drafts, unsold copies, while our provider of funds listened with half an ear and polished his nails.

'How much?'

'We'd have to be sure of providing at least four issues…'

'How much?'

'If we reckon on a circulation of ten thousand, which will certainly be exceeded…'

'Lola! Pass me my chequebook.'

It was the first cheque that I had seen anyone sign. Rather as if this man had just made a banknote.

'Here's 20,000 francs… Come and see me again later…'

Deblauwe took the money without a quiver, so that you would have thought he had been doing nothing else his whole life.

'Of course, you are free to write anything you want. But I would prefer it if you did nothing political.'

'Nothing political,' replied Deblauwe.

'Nothing political,' I swore.

'As for my name, on no account must it appear. There are two of you editors. That's enough. I'm doing it for fun, and if they knew that I was in charge of a magazine, the Romanian government would probably be amazed…'

The most extraordinary thing is that I still had not wondered why this man, who was apparently one of the greatest lawyers in his country, was living in a furnished apartment in Liège, and why, all of a sudden, he gave us 20,000 francs to found a satirical magazine.

He was just a patron of the arts! The kind of person who was capable of offering you some 'cordon rouge' at eleven o'clock in the morning, as he got out of his bath, and sign a cheque for you without even rereading it.

'By the way, I myself might write a little article from time to time…'

'That's only natural. As many as you'd like.'

'It would be quite rare… However, I've got two or three topics in mind… Besides, I won't sign them…'

'As you wish…'

I was restless… I dreamed of only two things: cashing the cheque at the bank and renting an office that would become the editorial offices of *Nanesse*.

'You'd also have to have some cartoons…'

'We've already thought of it,' declared Deblauwe. 'I've already acquired the best caricaturist in Liège…'

Leaving the room out of *A Thousand and One Nights*, I was not drunk. Nevertheless my head was spinning a little. We had not gone five steps along the pavement when I exploded with enthusiasm, while Deblauwe, impassive, with his hands in his pockets, his walking stick raised for battle and his briefcase under his arm, whispered to me, 'Careful! Maybe he's watching us from the window…'

Of course! We should not give this man the feeling that he was a mug, that he had, all in all, just made us a gift of 20,000 francs, for nothing, for the pleasure of seeing the founding of a satirical magazine and perhaps of writing an article in it from time to time.

Well, having turned the corner of the street, I was free to gambol as I wanted to.

'I was going to ask him for 10,000,' Deblauwe admitted to me. 'We can start publishing in fifteen days from now. Start by writing about thirty reports.'

'About what?'

'About anything. It's not important.'

The cheque was deposited, but I hardly saw the notes that they handed us in exchange, for Deblauwe decided that he was the one who would be in charge of the funds.

As for me, while waiting for us to make some profits, I would make thirty centimes a line, double that allotted me by my newspaper.

In other words, as there were four pages to fill, I could start literally manufacturing money! I learned how to do it immediately, went into a café, and asked for some paper and a glass of beer. A quarter of an hour later I had written a hundred lines of reports. That was: thirty francs!

Thirty francs in fifteen minutes, that makes 120 francs an hour, and I announced coolly to my friends, 'I'm earning 120 francs an hour!'

Without including my share in the profits from *Nanesse*, when they came in. It has to be said that there were still some young people who liked to shut themselves away in the evening in the *caque*, and discuss stupid topics by the gleam of a candle while drinking poor alcohol!

As for me, the following day I took my thirty reports to Deblauwe, plus a humorous story, and, full of largesse, he paid me the exact sum straight away, for he still had a part of the 20,000 francs in his pocket.

I said nonchalantly to my colleagues on the Liège press, 'You know, if you have an idea for a funny article, give it to me. I'll pay thirty centimes a line.'

And I bought myself a bowler hat. I had never worn a bowler hat, but I regarded it as going well together with my new dignity and my gaiters. I was taking a real risk, but only in a tête-à-tête with my mirror, with a watchglass by way of a monocle. No!...

It was going too far, especially at one go...

I went to a real nightclub, where I had never set foot before, a club with wall seats in strawberry-coloured velvet, a jazz band, an American-style bar, and pretty women dressed in silk.

There would be no more running after little unhealthy girls on Le Carré, and no more taking some indifferent and docile Charlotte type behind the church of Saint-Pholien.

I was surrounded by women, real ones, like Lola, and at three o'clock in the morning I took a room in that same hotel, where, during my first banquet, I had caused such a scandal.

When the first issue of *Nanesse* appeared, my mother declared to me, 'You should be ashamed to write for such rubbish!'

On this point she was exaggerating. Admittedly, the texts and drawings were not excessively conformist and, since it was necessary to make jokes at all costs, we were forced to do so at the expense of respectable people and institutions.

But, all in all, there was nothing really malicious in it, nothing but one thing that bothered me, a small article, on the fourth page, which I had not written and which Deblauwe had not talked to me about, an article moreover that I reread without managing to grasp its meaning.

Is it true that a certain M.T.... well known in our town...

Who was this M.T....? And why was someone giving us to understand that some day or other he might have an unpleasant surprise? Why did he quote such a commonplace proverb: 'All that glitters is not gold'?

I said to Deblauwe, 'It's not funny! It does not mean anything!'
'You think so?'
'Yes, I certainly don't understand...'
'Maybe there are some people who understand!'
'Was it you who wrote this piece?'

'Fool!'

Oh, yes, what a fool I was! It was the first article by our provider of funds. And I was still naive enough to shrug my shoulders and murmur, 'He knows nothing about journalism. Fortunately it will pass unnoticed, and besides there are other good reports.'

Mine in fact! Real articles, which revealed that the tramway stopped at such a place, because the bistro opposite belonged to a town councillor, or, what is more, which demanded that household refuse be removed before ten o'clock in the morning...

Could I have known that the sole *raison d'être* for *Nanesse* was precisely this stupid little piece on the topic of M.T.... and that the only reason our Romanian had travelled across Europe was to write it?

Could I have guessed that Deblauwe had told him, 'I've got a nice little colleague whom we can catapult into the post of editor-in-chief and who will fill up the four pages for us very cheaply.'

Even less could I imagine Danse, in his bookshop, going through our rag with a fine-tooth comb, and creasing his eyebrows as he read the brief article in question, and that, sensing what was going to happen, he was already planning to buy out *Nanesse*, which would get him condemned in his absence to a two-year prison sentence one day.

Intoxicated with the spring and with fame, I was living through an exhilarating period of clean nails, cosmetics and mouse-grey gaiters.

5

Very much later, in Paris, I was to get to know editors of the same kind of magazines as *Nanesse*, more important ones of course. And now, when I compare him with them, I am really forced to admit that Deblauwe was really cut out for it.

At that time indeed I fell for it, and I was flattered by the trust shown by my co-editor in my young age and inexperience.

'Hey, Deblauwe. I think I've got a marvellous idea...'

He continued to consult his files.

'To demonstrate administrative indifference, I'll go to the Town Hall with a barrow and carry away a crate one metre by one metre fifty, which must be heavy because it contains periodicals. I'll carry this crate myself on behalf of the burgomaster to the local library, where it should have been for the last two years.'

'Fine...'

I carried out this plan moreover, which is not important. What matters is the total indifference of my associate towards everything affecting editorial matters.

'I wasn't too hard in my article about the Theatre Royal, was I?'

He did not even know that I had written an article on the topic. As for him, he did not write a line. He left it to me to fill the four pages and if you saw him at the proof-setting table it was only to make sure that an advert had been well placed.

To tell the truth, I realise now that he had the makings of a real newspaper editor for that special genre of magazine, and he had understood that his place was not in the office – where nobody came! – but in the cafés and restaurants, perhaps also in official anterooms. In any case, editors of that ilk, I mean those who get into trouble with the law repeatedly, work exactly the same way in Paris and have the same contempt for these cock and bull stories that we scribble away at before reeling them off.

If I remember rightly, our second issue did not contain any article by our provider of funds, who did not even have the curiosity to take a glance at the magazine's premises.

'He'll have to let us have ten more notes this week,' Deblauwe announced to me calmly. 'The coffer is empty.'

And he went by himself to visit the Romanian, but came back with a slightly worried expression.

'I'll get the cheque on Saturday… He has to get the dough sent from Bucharest…'

On Saturday, the man only appeared in the afternoon, when the banks were closed, and he asked Deblauwe to come back the following week.

This time there was a new little article as incomprehensible as the first, which went roughly like this:

We happen to know that an unprecedented scandal will soon break in Liège, throwing a particularly harsh light on the lifestyles of certain high class families, who believe that money puts them under the protection of…

On Monday, I would have still very much liked to have been paid for my two or three thousand lines.

'I went to him,' Deblauwe said to me. 'He's left for Anvers. They think he'll come back tonight or tomorrow…'

On Tuesday, the paper dealer comes to the office, makes himself comfortable, with a threatening manner about him, and announces that he will only leave when he is paid.

'I'm going to go and get the funds,' Deblauwe announces to him. 'I'll leave you with my colleague.'

That was me! Hours passed. From time to time, the chap grumbled disagreeably along these lines: 'If you think I'm going to let myself be pushed around by adventurers?'

Or something like, 'Do you hope to wear me down? Don't count on it. I'll phone if I need someone to bring me a camp bed.'

As night was falling there was a telephone call from Deblauwe.

'Is he still there?'

'Unfortunately yes!'

'Too bad for him. The Romanian hasn't some back...'

'What is it?' the dogged creditor asked me.

'Well, there you are! The call was to say that no money will be available today...'

'And if I smash your face in to teach you some manners?'

'In the first place, that wouldn't get you anywhere. Secondly, it wouldn't be smart, because I'm also owed some money.'

Only on Thursday did Deblauwe confide in me that the Romanian was neither in Anvers nor in Liège, but had left Belgium for good for his native country.

'Prepare some copy anyway. The magazine must come out.'

'But as the paper dealer and the printer...'

'Don't concern yourself about that. Prepare some copy.'

Yes, Deblauwe had what it takes. The proof is that *Nanesse* came out again and that for many weeks the paper dealer continued to give us credit. I even think he invested in the business.

I never learned the whole story about the Romanian. All that I learned later was that a few years previously, in Switzerland or on the Riviera, he had managed to marry the heiress of a high-class family in Liège, and that it could not have taken them long to realise that he was nothing but an adventurer.

They sued him for divorce and got it. The man had tried again nonetheless, and decided to live from then on at the expense of the family in question.

One evening he had met Deblauwe in a café – it's incredible the number of people that Deblauwe got to know in cafés! – and the idea of the magazine was born.

Had he pulled it off? And did the Romanian's departure mean that the family had got their act together to get rid of him? If that's the way it was, it was obvious that it had cost him his 20,000 francs.

But had perhaps the police also discreetly made him realise that the air was a good deal more healthy on the other side of the frontier?

I never found out. I assume that Deblauwe had more information. Once again he was a real editor-in-chief, and he did not whisper a word to me about it.

The fact remains that, in the third week, I went into our office, embarrassed and blushing, because I was going to tell a lie.

'I say, old friend… Something very annoying has happened to me… The editor-in-chief of my paper has given me the choice: either work with him, or write for *Nanesse*… You must understand…'

He hardly raised his head to glance at me in gloomy indifference. And I launched into new explanations, which he interrupted suddenly, shrugging his shoulders, and grumbling without anger, 'You fool!'

What did it matter to him whether I went or stayed, since the only thing I could do was write. Weren't there fifty young chaps like me in the town who could most likely fill for him all those columns of humorous reports at thirty centimes a line?

This was proved by the fact that *Nanesse* continued to come out. And the person who replaced me in the role of churning out mindless copy did not ask for one sou for his contribution, quite the contrary: his name was Hyacinthe Danse!

I would have sworn, at that time, that everything that the young girls told us during the war about the lustful second-hand bookseller had only ever happened in their imagination. Indeed Danse was the perfect embodiment of a type of man that we knew only too well, which all those who belonged to a provincial newspaper knew.

I remember his first visit to the daily that I belonged to. I'd swear that he was in a morning coat, at any rate in an embroidered jacket, and that he was wearing the ribbons of several foreign orders. To get into the editor's office, it was necessary to cross the office where several of us writers were, and it was to me that Danse, self-important, with his aggressive paunch, held out his visiting card. After this he sat down and placed his hat on his knees, like a man who was accustomed to wait.

His card alone was sufficient to classify him in that category of especially tenacious beings who attack the editorial offices of newspapers with tireless patience:

HYACINTHE DANSE

Poet and dramatic author
First Class Graduate of the College of Saint-Servais and
of The University of Liège
Member of the National Belgian League
Former Member of the French Friendship Society

We knew others who would come back periodically, wait for hours and hours, and at the end of the day, speak to the editor about a question concerning waterways, unless it be to propose a new maritime canal, and they all had the same dignified manner of waiting, indifferent to our ironical looks, and to the time that slipped by and to the comings and goings around them.

'What does he want? Ask him,' said the editor.

And I went back towards Danse who recognised me vaguely as one of his clients.

'Say that it's on behalf of the French government,' he replied, showing me an envelope with a heading referring to the Élysée and bearing his name and address.

He was received. Half an hour had passed when our editor came out of his office and whispered to me, 'Come in after a few moments and announce that I am urgently requested to go to the Provincial Government Office. It's impossible to get rid of him!'

What a liar, a liar and a half! For, of course, Danse was not charged with any mission by the French government. He had simply come to explain that he was the author of a series of poems to the glory of certain places, which, like Yser, the Marne, Verdun and the Bois de Dames, deserved to survive in human memory.

He left with dignity as he had come, and my editor called me, and, with a sigh, held out to me a roll of paper.

'Have a look at this... Make any corrections if it is necessary... We'll have to publish it in a corner of a page, in small print... I couldn't get out of it any other way.'

It was an ode. And, a few days later, we noticed that he had given one of them to a liberal newspaper and another to a socialist newspaper, so that his name appeared everywhere at the same time.

'Bah! This way, at least we're rid of it...'

This was completely wrong. One was never rid of Danse and irony had no more hold on him than boorishness. And on the occasion of the visit of a famous foreign person, wasn't there a buffet lunch at the Town Hall? In the first row you could catch sight of Danse, big, fat and stately, who would flood you with a fluid smile and hold out a limp hand to you.

'What! Are you here?'

'As you see...'

We asked one of the burgomaster's deputies, 'In what capacity was he invited?'

'I've no idea. Ask the general secretary...'

And the general secretary did not know either. He believed that Danse had come in with a press card. It has to be said that we were stupid enough to laugh at it, while it was he who had the better of us! For in these ceremonious receptions, not only persons of secondary importance were on parade, but they continued to fête such people as Poincaré, Marshall Foch, and kings and princes, whom Danse always found some way of getting close to.

'Excuse me, Sire! Will you allow a Belgian poet, who is preparing a book to the glory of your country, to ask Your Majesty for the honour of your autograph?'

The pen was ready, and the paper too. At such moments, in the soothing warmth of the speeches, banquets and ovations, a few more words don't make any difference: 'To the great poet Hyacinth Danse, with all my affection...'

And what if there was a procession through the streets of the town or an unveiling of a monument? I don't know how he managed it, but he always had an armband and walked at the head of the column, with such an important air that it was to him that people turned to ask for information.

'Who is it?'

'I don't know... He must be one of the committee...'

He came back to the newspaper five times, ten times, always on different pretexts, and each time he found some way of getting himself received.

'I'm leaving tomorrow for Germany, where I have been charged with a mission. Don't ask what the mission concerns, because I would not be able to give you a reply and perhaps that is sufficient for you to understand. If you were interested in receiving articles on what's happening over there, I am entirely at your disposal.'

It took a long time to realise what he really wanted: a press card, in his name, with a photograph and stamped, a press card that would allow him to do God knows what!

Our editor was prudent. But another one, I no longer remember which, fell for it, and Danse got his press card, and, if my memory is correct, even put himself forward as a candidate to the union of journalists, and I am not sure that he did not become a member for a while.

The time when we laughed most about him was when he claimed to be able to make a newspaper successful solely by creating for it a daily astrological column, which he prided himself in being in charge of, and today, twenty years later, all self-respecting newspapers have their astrological columns and even ones on palmistry!

He must have had an impressive budget for the stamps alone, for he wrote to anyone constantly and even when there was no occasion for it, with no concern about being ridiculous.

Dear Minister,
I have just learned that the project of enlarging the Campine canal has been decided on in the most recent cabinet meeting. As a specialist in these matters, having grown pale with pondering the problem for years and years, I take the liberty of...

There followed some suggestions that were more or less intelligent, then the signature, followed by all the gentleman's titles, and finally a postscript, reminding the reader that he had received expressions of thanks from several foreign governments for the advice that...

I don't know what proportion of the letters remained unanswered. But we may suppose that only one in ten times would the minister, or the sovereign, have said to his secretary, 'Write a few words in reply to thank him... You never know!...'

That's how Danse received a fine official missive that he could cite from!

Ditto for the banquets. It was no good his being in fine clothes with ample decorations. It still happened from time to time that a grumpy organiser would come up to him and ask for his invitation.

Did they throw him out? And after that? Is there any enterprise that does not entail risk? What is more, honest people feel obliged to do it discreetly, and it is the person who throws the other out who is the most embarrassed of the two.

'I shall complain to the proper authorities,' he said with dignity as he withdrew.

Probably, since that period, he, who would one day claim that he had always been mad, had taken a secret pleasure in hearing one of us little morons declare confidently: 'He's a nutcase!'

What I find amusing is that he approached Deblauwe of his own accord, as if he had realised…

And what I find incredible, afterwards, with hindsight, is that at the time when these things are happening, nobody notices it, not even the most intelligent.

Not only does nobody notice anything, but they lend a hand without realising it. My editor, the most honest and most scrupulous man in the world, published one of Danse's odes in his columns to get rid of him.

And Deblauwe, in another newspaper, still wrote his daily piece, did reports on dogs that had got run over, and attended official banquets, while we all knew that he had a woman in a house in Barcelona.

He did not mind reading in front of us the letters that he received from her, written in pencil on squared paper, and we imagined what she could be telling him.

'Is she OK?' we asked anyway, as if we had been asking for news of his mother.

'She's getting along!'

Now, in the same newspaper to which he contributed, they pushed their concern for etiquette as far as banning the words mistress, pregnant, giving birth, and God knows what else, and the popular serials, which were not signed Henry Ardel,[22] could not have outdone those of this author for audacity.

I was not there when Danse arrived at the office of *Nanesse* and I do not know what the two men could have told each other. However, I imagine that Danse did not need to present himself any differently to when he visited us.

'I thought that perhaps, given my knowledge of life in Liège, I could be useful to you in providing you with a few reports... Of course, for me it's not a question of money... I'm a poet and bookseller... I've contributed to the leading journals.'

And I'd swear that Deblauwe said to himself, 'This chap's even more stupid than Simenon, because he doesn't even ask for money!'

How could he mistrust him? He had such confidence in him! And he held on, with his magazine, despite the failure of his Romanian backer. He obtained subsidies from certain commercial firms, theatres, cinemas...

For my part, being no longer the main writer, it was inevitable that another period should succeed that of mouse-grey gaiters and collars with broken tips.

I would gladly have returned to the *caque* and I think that, in reaction, I would have put up with a shaven head and long nails.

Only there wasn't any *caque* any more and, for several months, the exchange rate of the mark would take precedence over all other topics of conversation, including Plato and Saint Francis of Assisi.

'When are you going there?'

'The day after tomorrow... It seems that Wednesday is a good day... They forecast that it'll fall again...

The trains for skiers in recent winters are nothing compared with those trains, where there was not even any more standing room in the corridors. All classes were mixed together, ordinary people, professional traffickers, those who dealt in eggs and butter and those who only dealt in gold and in precious stones, middle-class women who needed a fur coat and 'first class' people who put on a casual air.

You set off in old clothes, old linen, worn-down old shoes, and from the station at Aix-la-Chapelle or Cologne on, there was a rush to the shops, where, with every hour, and sometimes ten times an hour, the shop assistants had to change the price tickets.

You met each other again in the same streets, and gave each other tips.

'Over there, on the left, near the cathedral, there are some amazing suits…'

When you arrived you were dressed in blue. At midday you were in grey, with a new suit paid for with a few million marks. One hour later you were sporting a moleskin hat and on the stroke of four o'clock you were waddling around in a coat of combed wool. As for everything that was hidden underneath!… Pieces of lace, silk by the metre, watches and pendants, and God knows what else!

You called out to each other from one pavement to the other shamelessly, without caring about those Germans who were watching you and who did not even have the courage any more to try to appear ironical.

'I've just worked it out… At the "Kaiserhof", for thirteen centimes you can dine with maître d'hôtel, wine waiter and everything…'

You leaped at the chance, laughed uproariously, and talked in high loud voices.

'Waiter! More caviar…'

What did it matter, since you had left with 100 francs in your pockets and had already dressed yourself from head to toe.

Of course they were clothes you weren't used to, in iron greys and rather odd greens, hats that were too stiff, all generally quite formal things.

'How much did you pay for it?'

'Four million marks…'

'At what time?'

'Eleven o'clock.'

'At midday they asked me for five and a half million…'

And the women!… And the lads who looked for you, near the stations, to introduce you to their little sister!…

In the evening, you piled into the return train and everyone had something to hide. There were the organised gangs, parcels that passed from coach to coach, according to how far the customs inspection was progressing, chaps who clung on to the bogies, and teams of customs officers, some famous for their toughness, and others for their leniency.

'I go across five times a week, and I can tell you…'

The greatest revelation was that money is not something stable, which you can rely on, but that suddenly it is possible to starve to death with millions of marks in your pocket!

'You see! My uncle is a banker. He claims that the mark cannot fall any lower. Even the other countries don't want it to…'

'Should we buy them?'

'I got two hundred francs' worth…'

And we also got some, I admit. And the following week we went back to Cologne, for the mark had gone down again and we worked out that the stopwatch we had seen would cost no more than forty francs.

I met Danse in the streets of Düsseldorf. Deblauwe took the train like everyone else.

We all had greenish gabardines, the same cigarette lighters, the same silver cigarette holders, which had not been checked through, and the same propelling pencils. The ordinary people of Liège were of no interest to us.

It was in an inn in Aix-la-Chapelle where, feeling brackish, I was waiting for the train to depart. It was quite a bad moment to get through. Setting off in the morning, with pockets full of marks, you had the impression that you were going to be able to treat yourself to magnificent things and unusual feelings.

Now, the trip to Germany came to resemble more and more those endless wanderings that one makes in the evenings, with a shameful expression, eyeing the passers-by, following a silhouette for several minutes in order to cling to the footsteps of another, in the false hope of something completely new, and with the certainty of finishing always at the same corner, over there where three or four shadows wait patiently in front of the door of a shady hotel.

The mark fell sharply, but prices rose. And what could we have bought that we did not yet have? What is more, a frightening rabble of people invaded the 'swindlers' trains', and in the town they hailed you from afar, as one of their compatriots, so that in the shops you were almost afraid of speaking French.

I had a wristwatch, another watch with a chain, two or three penknives, some cigarette holders (but I only smoked a pipe!) and other useless trinkets. That day I was to run into a common woman, the like of whom I could have treated myself to without leaving Liège.

Since ten o'clock in the morning I stuffed myself with sausages – only because I had decided that in Germany you have to eat sausages – and I had a queasy stomach, bloated with beer.

It only remained to wait for the train, and cram myself into the corridors with people who had a bad smell and who addressed you familiarly without knowing you...

At the next table I noticed two young men of my age, two brothers, perhaps twins, for they looked alike in all respects. What struck me was their pale, nervous faces, their eyes reddened like those of Russian rabbits, and their bushy ginger hair. Below the table I caught sight of khaki haversacks that must have been army issue.

Then I heard the two brothers talking French. A little later we struck up a conversation and I was amazed to learn that, since childhood, they had lived less than three hundred metres from my home.

'You're taking the five-fifteen train back too?'

'No! We're going on foot…'

I found out a little later that one of them was seventeen years old and the other eighteen and a half. However they already had the self-assurance of grown men and a sort of haughty indifference and deliberate impassivity, which attracted me and disturbed me at the same time.

'It's wiser to "go through" on foot,' they confided in me, pointing to their luggage.

We had to have a drink. We were always drinking! I let the departure time of the train go by, and when night fell, my companions got up and took me with them to the edge of a forest, then along a main road. We walked like this for two hours, perhaps three. We arrived at Herbestal, the frontier town, and the two brothers, having done it regularly, made a detour and, as we approached the customs post, they moved forward by sneaking from doorway to doorway.

'How are we going to get back to Liège?' I enquired once the danger was past.

'It's easy. Follow us…'

I think I was trembling as much as and more than if I had been a genuine criminal while we were clambering over the fences and wandering among the railway lines in search of a goods train. Sometimes, when we heard voices, or caught sight of a shadow carrying a lantern over its head, we pressed ourselves into a denser spot of darkness and held our breath.

I was hoisted up into a wagon. It was three o'clock in the morning when, in Liège, we again had to use a trick to get out of the station.

Now, my two comrades, whom I shall continue to call the Two Brothers, as they have a well-known name, were boys from an excellent family and even had the right to a noble title. Their father, an industrialist, was divorced and was living with a very young woman. Nevertheless he continued to make payments to his sons and their mother.

'We're professional swindlers,' the lads explained to me. 'We work on behalf of a wholesale dealer in electrical goods. On each trip, we bring back up to thirty kilos of spare parts...'

They lived with their mother in a decent, respectable apartment in a middle-class area. They did not frequent the *caque* and had never discussed Plato, nor recited Verlaine.

The fact remains that several times a week, in the morning, the mother ran to the police station, where she was well known.

'Haven't you seen them?'

'No! Sit down! We'll ring up...'

The station sergeant telephoned round all the local police stations, certain of the fact that at one of them they would reply.

'Yes, they're here!'

'How much?'

'Two hundred francs. What's more, a woman claims that they stole her watch...'

The mother was also ginger-haired, still young but hardened, with many silver threads in her hair and an expression that was always anxious, almost wild, as if she had constantly sensed misfortune around her.

Dealers, and neighbours, both men and women, knew her.

'I need another two hundred francs... Listen! If you lend it to me, I'll pawn my sewing machine... Or else... Wait! I've only got this locket left... It's made of gold...'

She began to cry in front of anyone, cry mechanically like a leaking tap, talking to herself, and pouring out her moaning cries along the pavements.

At the police station she paid and swore that her sons were basically not bad, that they would mend their ways and that she was going to keep an eye on them more.

But she knew well that it was useless to give them a talking to. They merely shrugged their shoulders or, at the very most, grumbled, 'So much the worse for you! You shouldn't have brought us into the world!'

Why were they so miserable? For they were dreadfully miserable. I spent some evenings with them, always in the same places, and always in the same way.

What was it that attracted them all, men like Danse and Deblauwe, and kids like the Two Brothers, to that kind of atmosphere? Not vice, strictly speaking. If Danse experienced it, it was not in the brothels that he satisfied it. No more did Deblauwe. And the Two Brothers were not healthy enough to go for women often.

No! What they needed, all of them alike, was that atmosphere of weakness and hopelessness, those women in shifts, who sewed or knitted with great balls of coloured wool near the stove, that bad beer in dubious glasses...

Alcohol, as at the *caque*, served only as a first stimulation and so you could talk, say things that you had not heard anywhere else, talk to yourself, all in all, with a fixed stare, a bitter taste in your mouth, while some woman waited patiently till you were finished.

'What reason is there for us to be in this world?' I was asked by the oldest of the Two Brothers, who had a long head like the comedian Laurel and the same sad look. 'Who could tell me? Nobody! So why should we worry? We'll have to die some day or other anyway. We two have certainly got tuberculosis...'

They did not kill anyone! The fact remains that I am horrified when I recall the things they confided in me. But the bookseller killed three people. Deblauwe only killed one.

The Two Brothers would have been capable of committing more monstrous crimes, for they resemble in every trait those tragic adolescents whom the most compassionate jurors send to the scaffold without hesitation.

The mother made tearful confessions to mine.

'The older one came back again tonight... He smelt of alcohol... He told me that he needed money at once... I didn't have any more in the house... What if I told you that I go for weeks without eating any meat because they take everything from me?... But tonight he did not believe me... He threw me brutally out of my bed to look under the mattress... Then he threatened me... He hit me to make me tell him where I was hiding my savings... Yet, he's not a bad boy.'

I saw this woman dying, so to speak. I avoided her sons, but I sometimes met them and sometimes they came and found me at the magazine to borrow money from me.

They prowled around the town like two stray dogs, thin and aggressive, and I'm sure that they would not have hesitated to attack a passer-by if they had known that his wallet was full.

And all this for nothing but to go then and collapse in a certain 'house' and live there for a few days in a state of dazed stupor until they threw them out.

One morning someone came to inform my mother that theirs was begging her to go and see her. She did so and found the woman in her camisole.

'You've just got to dig out a skirt for me, any kind. This morning both of them came. As I had nothing to give them, they took the last of my clothes and my shoes to go and sell them. I can't even go out!'

Then still that leitmotiv: 'I swear to you that they aren't malicious. Some people advise me to make a complaint. I know that if they lock them up, it'll be the death of them.'

They died without that, both of them, with not much time between them. The older one, however, made an effort. One fine day he joined the colonial army and they shipped him off to the Congo. They shipped him off drunk, for he had received an enlistment bonus. During the outward voyage, he did not appear on the bridge a single time, as for three weeks he did not sober up and was ill.

At Matadi the leaders did not want him any more and he did not disembark, and came back as he had left, still drunk, still vomiting, to be returned, after a month or two of military prison, to civilian life.

Two years later, the mother finally died, forty-five years old, dried up and worn out like a very old woman, with just some moisture in her eyes.

At that moment, one of the brothers was in Paris, where he was prowling around Les Halles at night, and the other was in Bordeaux or Brest.

They were two young people from a good family, well brought up, sufficiently well educated and, all things considered, more intelligent than the average.

Later, while living in Paris, I saw the older one again begging, and, scarcely twenty-two years old, he had been affected by a nasty incurable disease.

'It seems that my brother died in Spain,' he informed me indifferently. Someone had told him, that in Barcelona…

Like Deblauwe. Thus, they all followed the same route, without knowing each other. So does a pre-established cycle of destinies exist?

The older one was without shame. He did not snivel. He observed, 'I'm in a rotten condition. They don't even want to look after me in the hospital any more. In the winter I manage to get to the South, because the most annoying thing is to sleep outside...'

I recalled the goods train where I had sat with them, my head placed near theirs on their haversacks...

'Are you married?... Are you happy?...'

No bitterness! He came back two or three times to ring at my door, and I confess that he ended up frightening me and that I wondered what would happen if, finding me alone, he noticed some money on the table.

I'm sure, now, that he would not have hesitated, and that you would have found him again, after committing his crime, in some disreputable street sleeping it off next to some girls, and making incomprehensible speeches to them.

I am also sure that for years his mother had been haunted by the same fear and that it was a relief to her to die other than at the hands of her sons.

Yet, as she said, they weren't malicious.

So I almost feel like asking everyone, 'How many murderers, how many failed murderers like the Two Brothers, did you know during your childhood?'

Didn't I receive the normal proportion of them? Was it the natural waste of a society?

Or else, why, in such a few years, in a given place, did I see Little K... die, know Hyacinth Danse and collaborate with Deblauwe, while I was on close terms with the Two Brothers?

The place, of course, did not count! There are no towns that are cursed, and mine is in any case a model of restricted petit bourgeois life.

Should we seek an explanation in the times? Are there periods of more intense ferment or moments when unhealthy trends are occurring?

Without romanticism, I incline to believe it, above all because in the youth that I never knew, I can find in almost all my friends that very something, less pronounced, that made of them what I have just said of the criminals.

Admittedly we read the Russian novels. But was that a reason for shutting ourselves up, at the age of sixteen or eighteen years, in squalid rooms, like the *caque* was, or in the back room of some second-rate brothel?

Where did we get this taste for the most fallen of women, for the most revolting love affairs, for those dribbling confidences, for that unsuitable elation between a couple of glasses of wine?

Was this fault due to Dostoevsky or Verlaine? Wasn't the fault due rather to that war that we as children had lived through without understanding it and that had left its mark on us without our knowing it?

I'm close to thinking this, because I knew Germany a few years after the dizzy period of inflation when you counted marks in millions and billions.

Now, the young people that I encountered, the ones who were the same age as we were after the occupation, also bore the stamp of a curse.

Did not they also, as we did, rent places for meeting together? They did not discuss so much there as at the *caque*, but they drank a lot there and in addition they used other drugs. Then, fiercely, almost scientifically, as we induced our crises of lyricism, so they pushed eroticism to the point of paroxysm.

It was the time, please remember, when they arrested all the pupils in one secondary school because a little girl was dead, a little girl who had been taken off somewhere by her brother with some boys and used by them all as a source of experiences.

It was the time when most of the trials on the other side of the Rhine had to take place in camera, and when not a day passed without the suicide of an adolescent.

Like the Two Brothers they said, 'What the hell are we doing in this world?'

They had seen their father ruined within a few days, and their mother take a lover in order to eat; they had seen fortunes made and unmade in less time than it takes to count banknotes, and they no longer believed in anything or anyone.

The occupying troops, in the shadows of the streets, with the gas lamps draped in blue, had taught us certain pleasures too early and we knew that women give themselves when they are hungry.

What am I trying to say? We had known a kind of poetry of hunger. We had seen, when the 'supplies' were restored, how a family divided up its ration of bread with the aid of weighing scales, each one jealously keeping an eye on the ration of the others; we had seen them counting the potatoes in the dishes and I made a false key to steal pieces from my parents' loft.

In this way differences in temperament between the children were revealed. My brother, for example, kept his bread ration for two or three days in order to be able, twice a week, to eat his fill, while we, having used our portions, looked away. Then, when the enthusiasm of victory was barely subdued, we had noticed that they were not arresting any of the profiteers, whom we had so often pointed out, but that on the contrary they settled into the position that they had won for themselves in the social hierarchy.

We had seen…

As well as this, what would become of those little starving Germans later, who, in Cologne or Düsseldorf, had looked out for us at the corner of the streets to sell us their sister, and who knew that, somewhere in the town, their mother was giving herself to men on the benches?

Under the occupation, had Danse been able to satisfy without fear his passion for not yet pubescent girls? And without the enthusiasm of the post-war period, could he have gathered, with a few poems, a whole collection of the autographs of famous men?

For Deblauwe, who came from Paris, while we had known nothing for four years of what was happening outside our frontiers, it was easy to appear to us like a great man, and his editors too were impressed.

I don't know if periods of order really exist or if it is an optical illusion, because, for my part, I've never known one.

When we were eleven years old, they hurriedly took us into the cellar because the town was being bombarded, and, suddenly, we heard cries: a hundred metres away from us, they had just gathered together randomly two hundred civilians and shot them against the houses.

When we were thirteen they claimed indulgence for us, saying, 'You have to be kind to them... they're so poorly nourished!...'

And they took us up onto the high ground, so that we would hear the big gun. Or else we went off to the countryside, and our mothers wore three petticoats on top of each other, in which they hid several kilos of grain.

They taught us to cheat, swindle and lie.

'If the Germans question you, you should reply that...'

They taught us to take advantage of shady corners, to live in the semi-darkness, to whisper. As we could not move around in the streets after such and such an hour of the night, we went to each other's houses via the roofs, in the moonlight.

And they gave us children the responsibility of carrying to the other end of town letters from the front, which, if discovered on an important person, would have got him shot.

Is this where our taste for mystery and squalor derives from? Is it from having lived for years in a state of elation, that we then felt the need for natural or artificial forms of elation?

Or was it simply a question of an adolescent neo-romanticism?

K... is dead because of it, hanged in the doorway of a church. The Two Brothers are dead because of it, one in Paris, and the other in Spain.

All in all, it is only K... who died in his home town. The others left it, following almost parallel routes. Deblauwe went to Barcelona and Madrid and Danse also went there.

Deblauwe killed someone in Paris, not far from the Gare du Nord, but it was at Saint-Étienne that he was arrested.

Danse first chose a small village in the French countryside, but his mysticism, unless it was his worry about saving his own head, drove him to return to Liège to accomplish his last act.

In novels all this is extremely simple, and the author, a real God Almighty, decides that So-and-So has done this for such-and-such a reason or for such-and-such other reason.

The fact remains that those were the people that I associated with at different times in their lives, people whose most outstanding movements I knew about, and with whom, what is more, I shared certain emotions, and about whom I asked myself anxiously: 'Why?'

If the Two Brothers had been in better health, would they have acted otherwise?

If they had lived together with their mother and father, would something have changed?

If Deblauwe had not found himself in charge of a blackmail magazine, would he have avoided his disgusting fall?

If Danse had not acquired the taste for questionable voluptuous pleasures and had not engaged in magic, would he still have killed his mother and his mistress with blows of a hammer to the head?

And if...?

It is a dreadful question, for then you begin to ask yourself: 'Why him and not me?'

Or again: If I had been tubercular, and my mother had been divorced…

Didn't we use to frequent those same vulgar houses and didn't we use to drink in the same way to give a more confused twist to our thoughts?

And didn't we make identical disillusioned comments on the artificial rules governing society?

What instinct drove me, for my part, to pass through each of these environments quickly enough to avoid getting stuck there and to wear sometimes light gaiters, sometimes a romantic felt hat? Why was it that, after two or three trips to Germany, I'd had enough of it and I avoided the Two Brothers?

Why?… Why?…

And why, when I knew nothing about it, did I leave Deblauwe at the exact moment when it was going to become serious?

For, up till then, Deblauwe, just like Danse, had been able to create an impression. When I split up with him, after such a brief collaboration, he was still taking part in organised society, and probably there was still time for him to stay there and escape his fate.

In the same way Danse had the option of staying as a second-hand bookseller, while engaging in his mania for writing poetry, collecting autographs, walking with a swagger in processions, and doing magic in the back of his shop, not to say cautiously satisfying his libido.

After the fourth issue of *Nanesse* – or the fifth, or sixth, I no longer know – it was too late. The die was cast. The two men, together, and then each for his part, would rush headlong into decline and crime.

6

It burst upon the town of Liège like an incongruous remark in the middle of a banquet. Everyone bought *Nanesse*, just to take a look at it, and even those who knew nothing about journalism sensed vaguely the enormity of the thing.

I remember that, during the two years following the war, Paris was flooded with small magazines, which were more or less bawdy, or saucy, as we used to say then. Now, some of these magazines were run by amateurs, who had come from business or industry.

There was no mistake about it, I swear to you! What had the appearance elsewhere of quite an inoffensive joke, became, in these magazines, plain smut.

Thus it was with *Nanesse*. The Romanian had published two blackmail articles in it and no one, except those concerned, noticed them.

But Danse was in a sudden rage, and all limits were withdrawn, those of ridicule, the obnoxious and above all of bad taste and vulgarity.

We are going to clean out the Augean stables...

At the time, Danse, from his first piece, indicated, higgledy-piggledy, everything that there was in the pigsty in question, everything he could put in, randomly, by chance, former disappointments or old grudges.

... Yes, Monsieur C..., spattering us as you go by in your sumptuous car, we will prove, with indisputable witnesses, that, when you were still a little employee of the firm of Z..., you owed it only to the generosity of your boss that you were not handed over to the law...

... We will relate how, by stealing a few stamps every day, you gave yourself a supplement of a hundred francs a month, which allowed you to...

After Monsieur C..., it was the turn of a judge:

... We will tell, Your Honour the Honest Judge, where, before she became your wife and held court in your drawing room, one could meet the beautiful Zozo, then a young kept woman...

There was a furore. It was an exploding bomb. It was Dante's hell recreated by a little second-hand bookseller who had heard of Savanarola[23] and who, being really crafty, nevertheless, with a wink to the crowd, wanted moreover to get some money.

And you, Local Councillor, do you deny that, each Friday, you go to visit a certain house in the rue de la Rose and that a certain lady, called Noémie, known as Mimi, not without reason, is better acquainted with your anatomy than anyone else? Will it be necessary to specify? Will you force us to defy the board of censors to...

The nice people were amazed. They had never seen such a thing. They wondered if it would continue. They wondered above all who could let themselves go in this way.

Monsieur P, the butcher... who exploits people, I warn you that I will tell all...

And the confounded man printed out the names in full and gave the addresses.

> We inform the population of Liège at once that the crisis will be resolved, if a certain pestilential stench were to remove itself and if certain refined people were to hold their noses at it...

What scenes took place between Hyacinth Danse and Deblauwe during those weeks of collaboration? I know nothing about it. I wasn't there. I was never with them in the small office where I had for a moment occupied an editor's seat, which was only a chair with a straw bottom.

As for Deblauwe, whom I continued to see every day at the central police station, where we consulted the police reports for our own reports on run-over dogs, he never talked about his collaborator, nor about his writing.

And I realise, now it's over, that if he possessed a certain gift of the gab he did not mention readily his own affairs or those of others.

Now, there are two kinds of people who maintain a haughty silence in this way about everything that is private to them: aristocrats, and members of the underworld. Besides, aren't they both in their way aristocrats, showing an equal contempt for the shrill emotional masses who know how to talk about nothing but themselves and their petty problems?

All in all, we had just lived through the years with Deblauwe. We had endless opportunities to meet together in the company of our colleagues. We saw each other again at the *caque*. Deblauwe was the complete opposite of taciturn and held forth more often than just when it was his turn.

The fact remains that all in all we knew nothing about him, less than about any one of us. That he had a woman in Barcelona and that he went there sometimes to see her? All right! But beyond that?

That, during the war, in the neighbourhood of the rue Montmartre, where he had been working as a journalist, he had frequented quite shady surroundings, among which could be found, curiously mixed up in it, the remains of the Bonnot gang,[24] and some former dynamite specialists.

If he had alluded to this sometimes, then it had not been to say anything about it in any way, but to deepen the mystery even more.

When I think about it, I am now sure that he despised us, all of us such as we were, writers or editors, poor artists or sons of the middle class, that he despised us without any need to reveal it to us, for he regarded us as not being capable of understanding.

At the time of the trial, his lawyer exclaimed, 'I admit, Gentlemen, that my client is a depraved person...'

I believe that Deblauwe was better than that. For to become depraved, it is necessary to have been a nice ordinary young man and it is difficult for me to imagine Deblauwe in that role.

Danse, if necessary, could have played the role of a sated bourgeois. But Deblauwe?

Nanesse was a scandal and he certainly was not proud of it. All the same he said nothing about it. He still stayed the same with his eternal fitted overcoat, his black felt hat, his stick, his leather briefcase and his fine moustache, which revealed his sharp teeth.

In fact, although he smiled often, I don't remember having seen him laugh.

Why would he have laughed?

We are proud to announce to our readers, that is to say the whole population of Liège, that we receive each day piles of stamped paper. It is proof that our clean-up campaign is affecting those people who should be affected. They believe they can stop the avenging broom by appealing to a legal system that is as rotten as they are, and whose turn will come in our columns...

I have known, since then, master blackmailers of another scale; Danse had at least one trait in common with them: an insuperable reluctance to show himself in public, where he would have run several risks.

I am certain that, in the evening, he pulled down the shutters of his shop himself and reassured himself that the bolts were working well. I'm certain also that, in the drawers of his desk, there was a whole arsenal and that, in the streets, he kept as much as possible within shouting range of the police.

Another clandestine birth...

Everything was suitable, stories about morals, minor fiddles and old malicious gossip going back twenty years. You wondered how one single man could have stored in his brain so many scandalous stories; you would have thought that since birth he had emptied all the chamber pots and all the wastepaper baskets in the town.

One morning, Deblauwe did not come to the police station. The following day, someone from his paper replaced him and announced, 'He's gone.'

'For ever?'

'You never know.'

'It's happened twice before already with him, and both times, he had announced that he would not be coming back any more.'

'To Spain?'

'Of course...'

As for *Nanesse*, Hyacinthe Danse was from then on the sole proprietor, the sole editor, the sole writer, the sole employee and at that moment he must have been convinced that his life's dream had at last been fulfilled.

Don't ask me why links can be found between cabarets like L'Ane Rouge, which can be found filled with the same cabaret artists in many provincial towns, and the boulevards of Barcelona,* nor why persons gather both here and there who have been noticed in the neighbourhood of the rue Montmartre…

It goes back, I think, to generations that have preceded us, and who, instead of invoking Plato and God the Father in the *caque*, printed libertarian magazines on the sly.

In Liège, when Deblauwe went off on holiday, I wondered naively, 'But why Barcelona?'

Yes, why not Nice or Italy? For I imagined that he was searching for sunshine and picturesque views.

In the same way, at L'Ane Rouge, the cabaret artists with greasy hair who sang the most vindictive verses discussed amongst themselves their Barcelona friends and pronounced the name as believers are said to pronounce that of Mecca.

Later, in Paris, among journalists and painters, I was to meet many friends who would say nonchalantly, 'Next week, I'm going to take a trip to Barcelona…'

Just as you could recognise certain political militants by their beards or their dandruff, and just as in the streets of a parish you could spot the factory board members in passing, so I ended up by sniffing out 'the Barcelona types' from a distance.

Alas! An adolescent nowadays will doubtless have some difficulty in understanding our mystical orgies at the *caque*, and for my part it is difficult for me to talk of libertarian bouts of drunkenness.

* This refers to pre-revolutionary Spain [*author's note*].

These are trends that pass quickly. Many of those who were with Little K... on that famous Christmas night that preceded his hanging are today calm, respectable men.

And I know many former 'Barcelona types' of that heroic period who are now editors of newspapers or industrialists.

Would they perhaps not recognise Deblauwe as one of them? It concerns them. Each one defends his own sphere of mysticism. Each one opens the gates of his religion to whom he pleases.

We, for example, don't recognise the Fakir as one of us, and if the death of Little K... leaves us with some remorse, we nonetheless claim that it was the Fakir who killed him.

'The Barcelona types' probably treat Deblauwe as we treat the Fakir and dismiss him to the ranks of common pimps.

The comparison makes sense. Little K... was a victim because he did not understand. He did not understand that, if we resorted to alcohol and ether to whip up our mysticism, if we conjured up Satan and the Good Lord, we should not have gone too far and taken the cause for the effect, and the effect for the cause, stuffing our noses with cocaine, nor should we have had ourselves put into a cataleptic fit every day.

What he did not understand, above all, was that, although we were sincere, we kept a clear eye on them, if only to exchange looks and take delight in the show.

It was exactly the same with Deblauwe. In other words he took everything one told him seriously. Deeply imbued with a mystical sense of freedom, which, as at the *caque*, was not without a certain tinge of eroticism, he blended everything together, principles and actions, the end that justifies the means and the indignity of work...

If we needed a disturbing atmosphere to get ourselves going, didn't the libertarians of his period meet together in attics or in some run-down slum dwellings, and weren't there also sexually exciting promiscuous women there?

He continued, and that's definite! He went all the way, like the Two Brothers, who could not live anywhere other than in a brothel, like others that I know *and who live there on a regular basis*, and go as far as renting a room by the month, not for dissolute reasons, but because they need that atmosphere.

Having failed in his career as an editor and then as an editor-in-chief of a magazine, Deblauwe went off to find his woman again in Barcelona, and there, sitting outside cafés, he was completely at his leisure to discuss pure politics, and the yield you could get from women in South America.

I don't know that part of his life very well. But I know Deblauwe. I've known others like him since.

First, he was in exactly the right place for him, aesthetically and morally speaking, sitting outside a café in Barcelona or Madrid. He had the elegance, the appropriate casual manner, and that sort of haughty discretion, that faculty of not being moved by anything, and finally those kinds of crude and brutal expressions that add a colourful note to a conversation.

At the *caque*, we recited from Saint Francis of Assisi.

Deblauwe could recite whole pages from *Thus Spake Zarathustra*.[25]

Why the devil did his lawyer speak of him as depraved? I almost said a little while ago that Deblauwe was an aristocrat, in the way that Little K… was a failed visionary, perhaps a sort of Verlaine or Villon.[26]

In contrast to them, didn't the grotesque sweaty face of that petit bourgeois Danse, trying his hand at various mystical things combined with shady deals, look like a caricature?

Deblauwe had developed the habit of spending his afternoons on the Ramblas, discussing, drinking and smoking, and enquiring from time to time, like a lord, about his woman's turnover.

Then, one fine day, he acquired two of them – two women!

Then he went to Madrid to collect money for South America.

Wasn't it in the name of their principles that Bonnot's companions decided to rob a cashier?

From both points of view, there was still the exhilaration of not being understood by the apathetic masses and of fighting head to head with the police.

There are some voluptuous experiences that we more timid creatures have not known, such as taking sweets to a friend in prison, or letting oneself be punished for another rather than talk.

All in all, everything is poetry... In poetry it's not the subject that is important: it's how you make use of it, it's what you yourself bring to it.

In Liège, Deblauwe must have taken inexpressible pleasure in despising us all, such as we were...

In Barcelona he could despise those idiots, who, being on heat, were driven to give money to a woman that would end up in his pocket...

In prison, he despised the cops and their uniforms, and that apoplectic judge who settled life's problems as if he knew something about it...

Even his slow decline could not have been without some charm. You can very easily get used to a low-class hotel and one day, when you are flat broke, you can find a certain excitement in sleeping on a bench after having queued up in front of a soup kitchen.

The 'decline', as the lawyer said, lasted a long time, seven or eight years, with its highs and lows, bursts of anger because someone pinched a woman from him and bouts of joy because he had found another who brought him a better return.

'Ferdinand Deblauwe, publicist.'

For he has a profession. An expert in his field, his past brings him a certain prestige and, however low he falls, he finds people who admire him.

Sometimes he contributes to newspapers and sometimes he passes himself off as a special correspondent of some Parisian rag, blending illusion and fraud in this way so completely that he can't tell the difference himself.

His clothes fade. He lets a small beard grow, which gives him more dignity. Wherever he goes, from then on, in the worlds that he moves in, he is the uncontested *intellectual*, who hands out advice to everyone.

During this time, that vulgar mass of viscera known as Hyacinthe Danse continues to fight against the whole town hiding in the back of his shop, mixing his low form of business with his concern to satisfy old grudges, attacking both judges and shopkeepers, trying sometimes to cause outrage and sometimes to obtain a bribe, getting paid for his attacks as for his silence.

For *Nanesse* was still coming out! As unlikely as it may seem, people prefer to withdraw their complaints rather than see their ignominious acts, for which they are threatened, brought out into the open. The authorities cannot do anything about it, for the chap is a devil at procedure and actions taken against him will last for years.

Everyone comes in for it. It started with the big fish. For lack of material it was necessary to fall back on the small fry, and these were not scandals any more, but malicious gossipings of caretakers.

Has your tenant displeased you? You can always write to *Nanesse*, which will devote half a page to the fact that the wife of the gentleman upstairs receives a young lover as soon as her husband reaches the office, and even that they always do it three times!

Have you fired your maid? Danse will be delighted to publish at length all the grievances she might hold against you, including your furtive fumblings in the back of the kitchen...

The two men, Danse and Deblauwe, follow different paths to end up in the penal colony, although for a moment their routes met.

It's true that theirs also met mine.

Was Danse attacked by the serious newspapers?

Immediately he publishes facsimiles of the letters that he has received, remembering that the same newspapers published his poetry.

He fights. He makes a noise. He wants to be talked about. He splashes around, puffing away, in a swimming pool that is too narrow for him.

As for Deblauwe, he dived down smoothly and none of his former friends has seen him come back to the surface. Some small magazines, in Spain or France, provide a refuge on and off for unsigned pieces of his prose. And he can always find a bed his size in the brothels.

His official mistress is now called Bergerette. The name of Danse's is Armande and has the same profession.

One of the two, only, will be murdered, but there will be other crimes, three, four, five…

Deblauwe has problems more or less everywhere, problems that cannot affect his spirits, since it can consist equally well of being treated as a suspect by the police as it can be due to his having deliberately put himself on the margin of society.

He becomes from then on one of those group of people, who, at the least pretext, are asked to show their papers, which are gone through with a fine-tooth comb, one of those whom one sends to the police station for the slightest thing and whom one sets free in the morning after a few pushes and kicks up the backside.

Does he think sometimes of the time when we did the reports together about run-over dogs, and when both he and I used to write in a virtuous tone:

Locked up: Last night, a woman of ill repute, a certain Emma P..., was arrested after having stolen the wallet of an honourable shopkeeper, Monsieur V..., in our town.

And here's another:

Bad boys: A certain Joseph N..., of no known address, has been arrested for a specific type of vagrancy.

That's exactly what he does, between Barcelona, Bordeaux, Clermont-Ferrand and Saint-Étienne: a specific type of vagrancy. With sometimes a little white slave trading to top it all, for he is attractive, a good talker, capable of persuading a stupid maid or a sentimental young girl to take a ship for the Americas.

One fine day, he learns from the newspapers that the editor of *Nanesse*, a certain Hyacinthe D..., has been condemned to two years in prison for blackmail.

Only, Hyacinthe D... was sentenced in absentia, for, well before the trial, he took the precaution of going across the frontier accompanied by his mistress.

What could Deblauwe do, apart from shrug his shoulders with an air of disgust, or else mutter between his teeth, 'Well done!'

What he does not yet know, what is more extraordinary, is that the other man will come to join him for good in his present profession.

Indeed, once in France, Danse has soon used up the little money he took with him. From now on, in order to live, there will be no other resource left to him than that of Deblauwe: to put Armande in a house on the rue de Caire, a house that runs its business firmly, especially on Saturdays, and where a woman who knows how to handle things in such a tricky business has no time to catch her breath.

The two men are unaware of each other. They are far way from each other, each drawing up his plan as best he can, each of them definitely feeling that the time for experiments is over and that it is necessary to stick to the present, above all to stick and even hang on with all one's strength to the sole source of income that still exists.

Bergerette... Armande...

Two men who have passed forty and the age of seduction.

Which of the two women will want to break free first?

Which of the two men will kill first?

7

The year 1931!... According to the accepted terminology, we are now men, although, for my part, I could never get used to the idea of being a grown-up.

There's no *caque* any more behind the church of Saint-Pholien. One of our most impassioned daubers runs a business for painting buildings, and on Sunday mornings he takes his little boy and girl by the hand for a walk in Le Carré.

Charlotte is married and she has a child: I have been assured that she has turned out to be as good a mum as anyone else – and I hope she has made up her mind to look after her appearance.

Of the whole class at the Academy of Fine Arts only two are left who do some painting, and one of them has even just been appointed a teacher of design.

Marriages, births and deaths, as always. And when, once a month or so, we meet each other, we talk just like my aunts: 'Do you remember Oscar? Come on, of course you do! The one who was always the first to get drunk and who never stopped vomiting... His first wife died of a tumour. The second is an employee at the Grand Bazar, in the toy department...'

'And Olga?'

'She almost died as well. Now, she's getting better…'

Everyone has become something, a cartoonist for a newspaper, a house painter, an advertising agent, a manufacturer of fizzy water…

Deblauwe lives in Madrid, with Bergerette, and his latest business cards bear the profession of engraver. Bergerette works as a coach in a nightclub and that's where she makes the acquaintance of a young Spaniard with a romantic name, Carlos de Tejalda, an employee of the Post and Telegraph Company.

Weeks go by. Deblauwe senses something, keeps an eye on his mistress and one fine day, she, who has had enough, declares to him, 'It can't go on! Tejalda loves me. I love him. We're going to live together.'

This Tejalda was another one of those who must have been a charming young man before he acquired his passion for dance halls.

From then on things happen in the most banal way. Or rather they do not. Two details at least will redeem them from banality.

First there is the reaction of Deblauwe, who remembers that he was a journalist, a master blackmailer, and has not lost his passion for writing. In the space of several weeks, he addresses to his rival no fewer than *eighty-seven threatening letters*, each one more specific than the last, and not leaving any doubt about his homicidal intentions.

He not only writes to Tejalda, but he also writes to his rival's bosses, that is to the head office of the Post and Telegraph Company, to put them in the picture. He writes also, in the same way, to the young man's family, and I can imagine him grim and furious, his felt hat looking despondent, scribbling away outside a café, trying to make a feeble point, to find the phrase that strikes home, the malicious remark that will hit the target.

I see him looking out for Bergerette at the exit of the establishment, where she continues to dance and I assume that Tejalda is there, his hand on the butt of his revolver, pushing his companion towards a taxi.

The couple lodge a complaint and on two occasions Deblauwe is arrested by the police, and detained for several days for minor offences.

This drags on for months. Having no more resources, he goes back to Paris, scrounging off his friends left and right, does a few odd jobs, but, in the evening, cannot stop himself sending off again some letters full of hatred to Madrid.

Is he really in love with Bergerette? Is he only furious at seeing his livelihood getting away from him?

All the more embittered as money fails him, he sets off for Madrid again, and tries to meet his former mistress, while she, seized with panic, persuades her lover to accompany her to Paris. Isn't there a kind of unravelling and comic illogicality in these chaotic comings and goings? There's this train by which Deblauwe arrives in Madrid, in third class... and the other train with which the couple flee but are held up for several days at the frontier because their passports have traces of scratching...

Tejalda is already no longer a nice young man, nor a post office employee with a passion for dancing. He is also going to discover the obsession with writing letters, and all those letters, at the end of the day, those of Deblauwe, those of Danse and those of Tejalda, will not have been written in such very different ink.

Indeed, the Spaniard, who claims the title of a society dancer and who frequents elegant tea parties in Paris, does his utmost to compromise the middle-class women who are over the hill, and it is to them that he will write, cynically, asking them for money in exchange for his discretion.

The couple live on the sixth floor on the rue de Maubeuge. Each of them works separately. Each of them spends the night away from home for equally professional reasons.

Deblauwe has to find the necessary money to return from Madrid to Paris... Everything goes from bad to worse and when he arrives he has to be content with a furnished room, way up high in the rue de Flandre, in the La Villette district...

Does he eat his fill every day? It's unlikely. And it is in a bric-a-brac shop that he will buy a raincoat for twenty francs.

On 26th July, dressed in this way, he goes to the rue de Maubeuge, making his presence felt to attract the attention of the caretaker, of whom he enquires whether Tejalda is still living in the building and if he is still with Bergerette.

'As far as the lady's concerned, I don't know, because I haven't seen her for several days... As for Monsieur Tejalda, he must be in.'

After which the caretaker doesn't give it another thought. The following day she is not surprised at not seeing her tenant. Only on the 30th, after having vainly rattled his door, does she decide to alert the police station, and, a little later, they discover the corpse of the Spaniard, who has been killed by two bullets at point-blank range and who died four days ago.

'The corpse of a society dancer has been discovered in the rue de Maubeuge,' state the newspapers.

'The hypothesis that it was suicide is being considered'...

Bergerette makes people aware of her existence and maintains that Tejalda did not have any reason to commit suicide. Through her they learn about the existence of Deblauwe and the threatening letters, and the description of the man from Liège is sent out in all directions, for, on the same day as the discovery of the crime, he left his room in the rue de Flandre.

'A raincoat with three bullet-holes'...

Even if the affair is not sensational, the newspapers talk about it anyway and the raincoat provides a colourful touch. It's the garment that Deblauwe paid twenty francs for and that he left in his hotel room. Now, the material, on the level of the right-hand pocket, has holes in three places, as if three shots had been fired through it.

Isn't that exactly the way that gangsters do it, as we have been able to see for some time in the cinema?

Deblauwe will even provide an unexpected gag that the American scriptwriters would never have dared to invent.

Indeed the newspapers gradually stop mentioning him. The detective division of the police force and the Department of General Security[27] do not relax their efforts in looking for him for months, as much in France as abroad.

For a year, all men who have the misfortune to resemble Deblauwe vaguely are stared at, are questioned in railway stations and at frontier posts. The files in the garrisons are gone through with a fine-tooth comb more carefully than ever.

Has our former friend suddenly revealed himself, at forty-three years old, as a devilishly skilled criminal?

One fine day, when people are no longer thinking about him, it happens that at Saint-Étienne, while classifying files, a prison governor raises his eyebrows. For a long time he looks at two photographs, one full face and one in profile, and then the dactyloscopic prints of five fingers from one hand.

'Is this chap still with us?' he asks.

'Oh yes, Sir. He's still got three weeks to go.'

'How long has he been in prison?'

'Seven months, I think. I'll go and check…'

It is Deblauwe they are talking about, the Deblauwe that they were looking for everywhere, in Paris, in the provinces, at the frontiers and whose description they have sent to foreign police forces, the Deblauwe who, during this time, is quietly serving a light sentence in Saint-Étienne prison for an unimportant offence!

The murderer who, by being in prison, eludes all attempts to find him!

I read in the newspapers of the time that report the trial:

Deblauwe, completely white at the age of forty-three, and who wears a pointed goatee beard, has, in his appearance, nothing in common with the pimp that he is accused of having become.

He expresses himself in a gentle courteous way and talks of the duty he fulfilled during the war. He contributed to a magazine of the trenches, developed a taste for literature, took on the title of writer, or publicist to say the least, and called himself de Blauw.

He also contributed to miscellaneous editorial offices and founded various monthly reviews, which have nowadays died out: *L'Ane Rouge* and *Nanesse*, for example. None of his ventures thrived, and one can be very pleased that this is so...

There is also a photograph that shows him in the dock, very calm, as I have always known him, his head a little bent, with the attitude of a conscientious delegate at some political conference. If he were taking notes, you would almost think that he was attending some trial or other as a journalist.

'Please forgive me, Your Honour...'

There has always been a certain preciousness about him, and the goatee beard that he has let grow reminds me that in a certain period of our friendship I had nicknamed him Aramis, because of his feminine hands, his slight gestures, and fine moustache that curled up over his pointed teeth.

'Do you deny having written these threatening letters?'

'I do not dare to deny the evidence, Your Honour. Perhaps however a distinction can be made between the feelings one expresses at the height of a fit of jealousy and an act that might have been performed in cold blood, with premeditation...'

'You deny having killed Tejalda?'

'I deny it, Your Honour.'

'The caretaker and two women neighbours officially identify you as the man who, on the 26th, that is the day of the crime, asked if the Spaniard was at home...'

At this point there appears a smile that I know well, and a familiar movement to straighten the points of his moustache.

'I have often had occasion, as a journalist, to follow criminal cases and you know as I do, Your Honour, and no doubt better than I, the weakness of most testimonies. So it was, in 1896, in Vienna, as related by Hans Grotz, Professor of Scientific Criminology...'

I was not at the trial. I admit it straight away. I could have been there. I thought that there was a risk of Deblauwe losing his head and that I did not have the right to risk disturbing him by my presence, to distract his composure in the smallest way.

As for Bergerette, she was present, and for an obvious reason. Wasn't it thanks to her that the investigation had been directed towards Deblauwe and hadn't they been on the point of concluding that her lover had committed suicide?

With the examining magistrate she did not hesitate to call Deblauwe a pimp and to confess that she had supported him.

But in front of him she becomes flustered.

'You admit that the accused, after your breakup, hounded you, you and Tejalda, with threats?'

'He threatened us, yes. But…'

But what? What is she going to say while he remains impassive in the dock?

'If he had wanted to kill, I think he would have done it earlier, already in Madrid, where he had the opportunity a hundred times…'

'You claim now that he is innocent?'

'I believe that our breakup dates back too long a time to have inspired still such an act…'

Deblauwe does not smile. I've always noticed that he has this distant air towards women. She is the one who is more disconcerted and feels the need to add, 'I insist on saying that *for me he has always been the most charming man that could possibly exist…*'

Now there's the raincoat! Deblauwe will probably say that when he bought it for twenty francs the garment already had the three holes in it. The bric-a-brac seller cannot remember it and is rather inclined to defend his merchandise.

There are also the caretaker and the two women neighbours. Now, at Charleroi, where Deblauwe claims that he was at that moment, nobody remembers having met him.

There is talk of him being depraved. I am sure that he does not care about that, and that the word only brings a contemptuous pout to his lips.

There is talk of brothels that he frequented and of all the jobs he has done. I think he would gladly boast about them!

The good-natured people of the jury look at him strangely, starting at every immoral detail that is disclosed to them. Then they withdraw in a dignified way. Then they return, a little redder, and their chairman coughs slightly before reading: *Yes* to the first question; *no* to the second.

They did not want to have his nice head with its goatee beard and they kindly ruled out premeditation.

'Twenty years' hard labour and twenty years' residence ban,' announced the Chairman of the magistrates.

And that's all! At least that's all for the jury, for the magistrates, for the journalists and for us. A door opens and Deblauwe disappears between two guards.

But for him, it's not all. All in all it's only beginning. If we work it out: at the age of sixty-three, or even much earlier if he behaves himself…

I bet that he will be exactly the same person, with his ironical look, his immaculate goatee beard, and his fine white hands. For over there they won't of course put him to work breaking stones on the road. They will find work for him in the office or the infirmary. He has an admirable way of telling stories and I would swear that he will make a good impression on those administrators and will become a sort of personality.

Who knows? Won't the idea occur to him of running a penal colony magazine using copying gel?

I was present at the departure from Saint-Martin-de-Ré. Amongst others there was Doctor Laget, dressed in an elegant brown golfing outfit of English woollen cloth. All the time during the formalities, in spite of the onlookers, of the film cameras, and despite the chains that he had on his hands and feet, he continued to look like a man of the world, to the extent that you would have sometimes said that he had a silly smile on his face, while his companions were already surrounding him with respect.

Why would Deblauwe lose a self-assurance that had never left him?

And if, over there, they get newspapers, what did he think when he learned a year later that Danse, in his turn…

For the latter things did not happen in the same way. And, at the hearing, nobody came to declare that *he had always been the most charming man that could possibly exist…*

It was necessary to use some tricks to get the accused into the Law Courts and without the gendarmes the crowd would have rendered the trial superfluous.

Round about the time when the trial of Deblauwe was proceeding, the former second-hand bookseller, who had been joined in France by his old mother, rented quite a spacious country house at Boullay-les-Trous, thirty kilometres from Paris, at the edge of the village, opposite the pond, where mornings and evenings the cattle drank.

He also gave his profession as that of publicist, which attracts so many adventurers.

And he was, in the eyes of the landlords, the most respectable man, well-nourished and easy-going, talking only of his acquaintances in official circles and of the sacrifice that he was making, for the peace and health of his mother, by withdrawing to the countryside.

The house was fitted out and, as in all villages, curtains trembled as people counted the pieces of furniture and ornaments, neither elaborate nor poor, but rather ill-assorted, that took up their places in the rooms.

A young woman was present at this process, an ordinary young woman, quite retiring, whom Danse introduced as a relative and who took the train back to Paris again straight away.

It was Armande Comtat, a resident in a brothel on the rue du Caire. This Armande Comtat, after finishing her work, took on the appearance of a shy petit bourgeois woman.

Books, many books, more books than the country people had ever seen, and, at the same time, strange objects that made you wince immediately, distorted masks like the faces of dead men, and skulls, and skeletal remains, which Danse unpacked with meticulous care.

The fact remains that he was *decent*, as they would have said in the South. Not proud! From the first few days, he went into the café ostentatiously, shook hands in the way of a man who likes people, and clinked glasses with everyone.

'I don't understand how people can be mad enough to live in the bustle of the cities!' he declared.

And, my God, the country people, who would have been really happy to live in Paris, were not angry to see someone who envied their lot.

'Do you know that one day, thanks to me, Boullay will be as world-famous as a pilgrimage site and that people will come here from everywhere, just as they go to Lourdes and Lisieux?'

That was harder to swallow. They looked at each other suspiciously. They coughed. Hm! What was he trying to say exactly? Was he starting to see things?

'You will see that which I foretell to you come to pass! I am the magus of a new religion…'

There would be talk about this under the thatched roofs!

'In any case,' they said, 'one fact is certain: he's good to his mother!'

'What's all this about this woman who comes from Paris every Friday and goes back again on Sunday?'

'Well, I was told that they slept in the same room… someone saw the light…'

'And even if it were true?'

Danse had one advantage: he was big, almost obese, and you don't mistrust big people, especially if they have a gleaming face with little pig-like eyes.

What is more, he listened, without ever interrupting, to everything that he was told, stories of scandals in the village and the surrounding countryside, the fiddles made by certain shopkeepers who went a bit too far and who priced their goods too high for the poor people.

'You'll see that one day all will change!' he promised.

He liked to stay on his doorstep, in slippers, his body draped in a huge brightly coloured dressing gown. You would have said that he was sniffing the air in little whiffs like a gourmand and that his eyes were caressing the scenery as certain enthusiasts caress a piece of Tanagra[28] or Chinese lacquer.

The pond pleased him, especially when a flock of sheep came down to drink there at dusk, and reminded him of certain pictures popularised though chromolithography.

'I shall call this house "La Thébaïde",'[29] he announces solemnly. 'And, due to "La Thébaïde" the village of Boullay will be illustrious in the centuries to come.'

To tell the truth, he did not have a sou. He had taken refuge in the countryside because he had no means of support and it would be easier to live there subsidised by Armande Comtat.

His mother did the cleaning. His mistress, during her weekly stays, gave him a hand and Danse was not averse to pottering around in the kitchen himself, and buying himself a piece of meat and cooking it.

'He's definitely a real eccentric!'

And for a country person this word explains everything! That's it, he was an eccentric! An eccentric who did no harm to anyone and who was really devoted to his mum.

If he did not always pay the tradesmen in cash, it was because he had his account in a bank in Paris and did not have time to go there to withdraw the necessary amounts.

'Next week I'll pay you…'

To show that he was not affected by this trivial matter and that he did not harbour any grudge, he doubled his order, as a man for whom it is of no importance.

'Think about what I told you: one day, "La Thébaïde"…'

And the country people did indeed see that day come.

8

I knew a restricted and sad chap, in a basement in the Saint-Martin district, who worked all day by the light of a 25-watt bulb, making packets, invoices, letters to be dispatched, sticking on stamps, writing addresses: he was his own supplier of funds, his own director, his own dispatch department, his own stock controller, his own errand boy.

The business consisted of publishing small libertine books with very titillating covers.

I knew another chap who was just as solitary, and just as dull, who did the same thing with packets and who, in the afternoon, went to the post office to cash surprising numbers of small money orders, which had come from all parts of France, Switzerland and Belgium. He had an advertisement published in the newspapers, which had been identical, even the numbers, for twenty years: *'Fifty francs a day, in your own home, through easy work. Complete equipment and instructions: forty francs.'*

All he did was send to the clients a box of watercolours, available in any general store, and some postcards to colour in with a note maintaining that at the rate of two hundred cards coloured per day...

I am sure that these two were the same breed as Danse. I can't explain it, but I feel it. There are kinds of loners who exist in this way, who never wash themselves thoroughly, who cook for themselves on a bad stove and who get fanatical satisfaction from exploiting the gullibility of the public.

Danse, who now called himself Armand Montaigle-Claudel, published a new magazine, which had only one issue and for which he was the sole writer. This magazine was called *Savoir*[30] and contained only articles on its founder, written by him under various pseudonyms.

This special interview, for example:

ARMAND MONTAIGLE-CLAUDEL INTIME

It was last August, at Deauville, that I had the good fortune to meet the poet and philosopher Armand Montaigle-Claudel and, deploying all batteries, to bombard him at point-blank range with my questions. For a long time I had wanted to find out, through the tough probing blows of a special interview, what kind of mind animated this legendary man. Smiling, and full of eloquence and wit, the Sage replied to my difficult questions, and was amused, he said, by this intellectual gymnastics by which he gambolled from memory to memory and from confession to confession…

'You have sworn to strip me naked,' he said laughing, 'but at least leave me my shorts, for, as you can tell: some ladies are watching us.'

I imagine him, writing his pieces with his tongue between his lips, in his grimy dressing gown. He puts the questions and replies to them.

What do you think is the best thing?
'To live! As long as there is life, all is possible!'

And he loves life so much, that, when he has killed two women, he will kill a man in Belgium, with the idea of saving his head!

Who is the philosopher whom you loathe most?
'Schopenhauer, the purveyor of tombs!'

And in a few months he will be the cause of slaughter.

Your most horrible memory?
'An autopsy, in the freezing month of January, in the cemetery of Molières.'

Soon, it will be he who will compel the doctors to carry out three autopsies!

What is your most refined intellectual pleasure?
'To look a fool in the eyes of an idiot.'

And in the court of the Assizes, he will overwhelm with insults the doctors who refuse to regard him as a genuine madman.

Your favourite pleasure?
'You're too inquisitive. But how about the affectionate kiss of nocturnal breezes, which are not unpleasant on the skin, on a beautiful summer's night?'

And the bodies of pubescent young girls we know, on cold winter nights during the war?

Who would you have liked to be?
'God! Think of all that knowledge! Or the sea, all that power! Or the ether, all that purity! But I'm happy to be myself and I thank Fate that I am what I am.'

Didn't some of our friends, at the *caque*, also envy God the Father?

What is suicide?
'Furnishing a poor brain, which had nothing in it, with lead.'

Will he never try to kill himself and will he prefer permanent imprisonment?

All possible subjects are reviewed, the arts, literature, the sciences, wisdom and the infinite, and then suddenly his crafty self manifests itself again, by posing to himself this question:

Do you like eating out sometimes?
'Yes. On condition however that the dishes are presented to me as a token of friendship, in a good spirit and with sincerity. I also like the surroundings...'

Advice to amateurs! The restaurant owners in the area are warned. Danse has not resisted the desire to arrange for himself several material benefits.

If there were a school of novelists, this issue of *Savoir* should become a sort of bible there. It can, in any case, remind us every moment of the poverty of our imagination!

Danse, hidden like a large rat in La Thébaïde, Danse to whom, every week, one of the girls from the 'house' comes to bring the money from her sessions, Danse who has to serve two years in prison in Belgium for blackmail, writes gravely:

An Idealist!
Peace for All the Peoples of the World

It is not only by the admirable and moving way that he looks into and deals with the pain, the anxiety and uncertainty of the dear people who consult him and visit him that the Wise Man of Boullay demonstrates his marvellous radiance and the generosity of his Idealist spirit. For him, the Absolute, the perfect Ideal is written with five[31] letters: Peace! And, to gain peace in his soul and know tranquillity in its absolute form, he tries hard, as far as the means at his disposal will allow, to inscribe these five letters in the hearts of those who consult him, as he would like to see them shine brightly in the four corners of the world, in Europe above all.

His famous Elegy to Briand,[32] which went around this Europe in ferment, show what peaks the Thought and Dreams of the poet hover over.

And if Romain Rolland became famous for keeping himself 'above the fray', what must the fame of Armand Montaigle-Claudel be like for trying to avoid a further disaster!

Immediately, as always, the crafty chap reappears, with a twinkle in one eye as he declaims, while looking at the purses of his clients with the other. Being a good retailer he issues references.

Congratulations to Armand Montaigle-Claudel for his poem in memory of Aristide Briand...

– Albert Lebrun
President of the Republic

... I was deeply moved on reading your elegy... You know well enough how great the fervour of my emotion is for all those who serve the pacifist ideal, for you to imagine the profound joy that I feel in reading such a literary piece, inspired by an equally generous and noble thought... my gratitude... my congratulations... my heartfelt appreciation...

– Raymond Patenôtre
Delegate for Seine-et-Oise
Minister of National Economy
Under-secretary of State to the Presidency of the Council

... I am deeply moved in reading your elegiac poem in honour of Aristide Briand...

> – *His Excellency Von Hoesch*
> *Former Ambassador of Germany in Paris*

... congratulations to Armand Montaigle-Claudel for the noble feelings displayed in his beautiful elegy in memory of Aristide Briand...

> – *The novelist Maurice Dekobra*

There are several pages of this in small print.

After which this piece of pure poetry, the little blue flower that, moreover, Danse signs this time with a female pseudonym and which, with disarming simplicity, he entitles: *A House*.

His own, of course! You can see the photograph of it, in the twilight, with the inevitable flock of sheep around the pond.

> It's very soft twilight in July, an evening in the Île-de-France, solemn and light, like a goddess, too beautiful, who, lowering her eyelids, would like to veil slowly her radiant face...

Further on:

> Doesn't the peaceful contemplation of this faithful and admirable photo of La Thébaïde in Boullay fill the eyes with a pure and magical enchantment, the heart with an exquisite and comforting impression of peace, the soul with sweet serenity, the mind with infinite certainty?... Time and space seem to be abolished before this evocative rustic picture, which could just as well be situated at 200 leagues from the tentacle-like towns as at six leagues from the frenzy of Paris!
>
> The appropriate residence of the poet, the wise man, the philosopher, the profound and subtle thinker, withdrawn far

from mankind, and yet so near to it by the Humanity of his art and whose pen, inspired by the never-ending dream and eternal Enchantment, excels, by sublime escapes, in conveying the imperceptible and divine countenance of the Unreal!

Now, the shopkeepers, for miles around, received a visit from Danse, from a less inspired Danse, although heartfelt, who declared to them, 'You know that my little magazine is going to come out. It will have a universal impact. It will attract a huge crowd in the region and you will profit from it. So it's natural that you help me with the initial expenses…'

Then, looking as though butter would not melt in his mouth, he said, 'It's obvious that I will be compelled to consider those people as personal enemies and at the same time as enemies of my ideas who do not give me a helping hand. In this case it may perhaps happen that I'll tell about certain things that I know…'

The country people also know some 'things'. They have found out about this woman who pays visits on Fridays and they are no longer ignorant about what she does in Paris, nor that she constitutes the Wise Man's sole source of income.

Some start by not greeting him any more. At the inn they talk of him with disgust, and one fine day a huge inscription can be seen on Danse's house, which has been done during the night:

THE HOUSE OF THE PIMP

A complaint is made to the mayor. One day when he is in town the latter speaks about it to the mobile police brigade, and one thing leads to another, and they learn that the famous Wise Man has been sentenced to two years in prison in his country.

The atmosphere has soon been transformed. The tradesmen refuse to deliver to La Thébaïde, and when Danse appears in the village all faces turn away, and the boys spit on the ground or let out animal cries.

The matter is discussed at the town council, which decides to ask officially for the expulsion of the undesirable person. They point to the fact that there are death's heads in his office and that he engages in magic. He makes threatening comments, talking of acts of revenge that he can carry out without leaving his study, just by incantations and mysterious practices.

A sort of cordon sanitaire forms around him, but he does not seem to notice it, and carries on writing, under the lamp, until late into the night. He takes the air on his doorstep, goes to Paris from time to time, dispatches ministerial mail, but receives much less.

The atmosphere is always that of this quite poorly furnished country house, with its untidiness, its faded curtains, its bric-a-brac and its old books. A mask of Beethoven is enthroned in the place of honour.

Later, some people from the village will make the journey to Liège to testify at the Assizes, and we will see the owner of the house, a little old lady of sixty-three, neat and slight, dressed completely in black, 'in the old style'.

'It's her, it's my landlady who betrayed me to my enemies!' Danse will exclaim furiously. 'She was jealous of Armande. She set herself against me. At sixty-three years of age, Gentlemen of the Jury, I let you be the judges of it!'

Then the sergeant in charge of the gendarmerie will explain: 'Danse at first led me to trust him. I saw him often. He talked well and knew a lot of things. Later I received complaints against him and complaints from him. His character had changed…'

The Chairman asks, 'Why did the people of Boullay feel aversion towards him?'

'Since he had set himself up as a specialist in the occult, they were afraid of him!'

And it is a display in which none recognise themselves. Danse said to the sergeant that the wife of the coal merchant threatened him with a gun. Danse added that the husband wanted to kill the President of the Republic and…

The owner of La Thébaïde says, 'I put up with all kinds of things. He was aware of long-standing problems. He paid his debts and bills on Fridays, after Armande's visit. But he did take care of his mother…'

And the people add:

'When his rage had passed, he was the best of men…'

If Danse had killed a few months earlier his crime would have closely resembled that of Deblauwe. But he had been given time to live in Boullay, and to write the first issue of *Savoir*.

And he had been given time as well to stir up against himself a whole area of the Île-de-France. Inscriptions soiled his walls. Noisy insults exploded and insulting words were exchanged.

So, then he turned out to be just as much a stickler for procedure as the country people and it was a question of who would take their complaint to the law the quickest.

'The butcher said in front of witnesses…'

'The other day, at the corner of the street, Danse threatened me that…'

The letters pour in from both sides. Relations get more and more ugly and Danse considers the whole population, outright, as his personal enemy.

But why the devil go and hide away in a village instead of contenting himself, like his 'associates', with a basement in the Saint-Martin district or in two rooms in the area round the République?

The Two Brothers, when they were just about emaciated and had slept two or three nights on benches, threw their mother out of bed and beat her, to squeeze a little money out of her, or else steal her remaining clothes from her, which they would sell again.

The signal for Deblauwe was the betrayal by his mistress, whom he could not replace, so much so that he also dragged himself along the pavements, looking at the cafés where he was prevented from sitting through lack of money.

The signal will be almost the same for Hyacinth Danse, whose issue of *Savoir* does not attract the anticipated pilgrims to Boullay.

Money is lacking. The populace is becoming more and more menacing. The old mother is afraid and perhaps she dares give him some advice?

There was no point in publishing so many testimonials by important persons, nor portraits of himself in the one issue of the magazine.

Sordid details provide the key to certain mysteries. Why, for example, will the coal merchant, in the mind of Danse, become the head of the conspiracy hounding him to his downfall? Because winter is not over and, in that isolated house, the heating is important.

It is May and it is still cold. All week creditors have come and gone, as usual, and also as usual Danse replied to them, 'Come on Friday afternoon and you will be paid...'

Now, though on Friday 5th May Armande Comtat comes to Boullay and brings a little money, she does not have the usual expression on her face, and she announces that she will not be able to stay till Sunday.

Why? She does not explain very precisely. She becomes confused. Her madam needs her. Her sister has asked her to come and stay with her for a night...

'You've got a lover!' roars Danse suspiciously.

'No! Why do you say that?'

Yet, it's true! She has a lover, and has had for several weeks already. Deblauwe's mistress met Tejalda at the dance hall where she was working. Armande Comtat met her lover in the house on the rue du Caire, in the form of a gentle and kind regular guest who promised to take her away from there.

On Saturday the 6th, Armande and Danse reach Paris and go different ways. In the evening, Danse, who has been brooding on his suspicions all day, phones the sister of his mistress and learns that she is not there, and then he phones the rue du Caire, where Armande is also is not to be found.

I imagine that at that moment he must have felt his legs go weak, that he must have understood that this was the end.

He sleeps or doesn't sleep in a furnished flat. In the morning, not having found Armande again he returns to Boullay and shuts himself away for two days, waiting for news.

Finally a telephone call from Paris.

'Hallo... It's me, yes!... I'm sorry, but it's not my fault... No, I'm not going to Boullay... It's better if I never set foot there again... It's finished, do you understand?... I love a man and he loves me... We're going to live together... You must forget me...'

He threatens. He cries. He wants to see her again one last time, just once!

'No! I feel it's better not to...'

The weather is showery. The sun is shining between the showers. Danse hangs up, rushes off to Paris, settles himself in a bistro opposite the house on the rue du Caire and spends several hours waiting there.

Towards evening, Armande goes out, goes a few steps, catches sight of her lover and runs away without him being able to meet up with her. So, he goes and rings at the house of the sister who looks at him, terrified, and who tries to calm him down.

Armande has indeed confided in her: 'He'd be capable of killing me...'

In the rue du Caire the instructions are quite strict: 'Don't let him in on any account!'

Once more he returns to Boullay, where, on the 9th, he receives a letter in which his mistress becomes as tender as possible. She seeks his forgiveness. She has found love. She is happy and she wishes him happiness... It's better for them to part in this way... She leaves him everything that belongs to her in Boullay...

Poor Armande, who believes she has escaped her fate! Her sister expressed it to her well: 'If you value your life, never see him again. He'll try to move you. He is capable of all kinds of tricks...'

She promised. She is completely preoccupied with her new love and soon she will be able to leave the house on the rue du Caire!

'...*one last time, once only,*' writes Danse, '*we will see each other outside a café... I must talk to you.*'

Is it to be believed that Armande, feeling dizzy, goes of her own will to face death? She accepts, without saying anything about it to her sister, nor to her girlfriends in the rue du Caire, who are all well informed about it and who follow this story like a newspaper serial.

The couple meet again, in the evening, outside a little café. Danse is calm. She tells him that she is pleased to see him so reasonable and he smiles a cynical smile.

'I can't stay in Boullay any more,' he says in a restrained voice, 'for too many things will make me think constantly about you there and I'm afraid of suffering. Besides, it's you that the furniture belongs to, as well as most of the things...'

'As I told you...'

'Listen! I've taken a big decision. In Belgium, I have to undergo two years in prison. I shall go there. In that way, during the two years, I'll be calm, alone with my thoughts and, when it's over, there will be nothing against me any more.'

Other customers, near them, are talking about this and that.

'Only one question worries me: my poor mother. That's why I thought that you could perhaps look after Boullay, where you have all your belongings... My mother would continue to live there... She will cost you almost nothing... As for me, during that time, I'll be in prison...'

He says all that with such resignation that she lets herself be moved to pity.

'I'll willingly look after Boullay and your mother...'

Two hours before, her sister had repeated to her, 'Above all, don't let yourself be dragged off there, whatever happens!'

She herself said, 'If he manages to be alone with me, he'll kill me!'

And yet, there, in the Parisian twilight, in front of cafés washed by the rain, she weakens, and it is he who talks, who talks in a hushed voice, as a man who hopes for no more than the peace of a cell, even if it is only a prison cell.

'So, at least, I will be reassured on your account and concerning my old mother... You were the only people I loved in the world... But, as you assure me that you will be happy...'

He must have found other words too, as, by ten o'clock in the evening, without warning anyone, her new lover, her sister, nor her madam, Armande makes her way towards the station in the company of Danse and takes a seat with him in a third-class compartment.

'We're going to settle everything perfectly, so that I'll have no more worries, over there, in prison...'

Did she perhaps cry seeing him so resigned? Does he not have enough generosity of spirit to suggest that his successor should enjoy after him the charms of La Thébaïde?

They alight at the little station, follow the dark roads, and catch sight of an illuminated window of the house.

Yet, if one is to believe what Danse will say later, Armande is nervous and, along the whole route, she keeps turning round, thinking that someone is following her.

Isn't it rather a case of believing that her new lover is following her to protect her?

The bistro is closing its doors. The farms have long since gone to sleep.

'You see! Mum is waiting for us…'

And they cross the doorstep, while Armande looks deeply into the night around them for the last time.

9

About that which will happen that night and on the following days, we only have the statement that Danse will compose for the purposes of preparing his case with self-indulgent meticulousness, insisting on certain details, making sure that the clerk of the court transcribes word for word without omitting anything. And it is this statement that will be repeated *in extenso* when he is charged.

Scarcely had the train left Paris when Armande started to appear strangely nervous, while I tried hard to reassure her. It was between the station of Boullay and La Thébaïde, while we were walking during the night, that her nervousness took on pathological proportions. It was as though she were HALLUCINATING (he insists on this word, which he sets great store by). She turned round all the time, started at the least noise, claimed that she felt she was being followed; for my part, I calmed her as best I could.

When we arrived at the house, where my mother was waiting for us, Armande wanted to go up to her room directly. The cat, a female, had an odd expression in its eyes that evening and uttered strange cries, which ended up making Armande beside herself.

'I swear to you that there are people prowling around the house,' she claimed, pacing up and down the room, without daring to go near the windows.

Finally, I went out and checked around. She accompanied me and her hand trembled on my arm. I could not reassure her as much as I would have liked, for we saw together the shadows flying away, and, when we went back in again, Armande was still as frightened as before.

It was then that she reminded me that prior to our move to Boullay someone had committed suicide, in that very room and in the bed that she now occupied.

She did not want to sleep there and we decided to spend the night in the kitchen, without sleeping.

Half an hour passed in this way. We each sat in our own chair. It was cold and Armande's teeth started chattering.

At half-past midnight, she cannot stand it any more and decides to go to bed. I follow her and take my place beside her in our bed.

Some minutes pass, in the darkness, and suddenly Armande throws herself against me. She goes sort of mad, shouting out that there are people outside, at the front side, and that she is sure she has heard a noise.

To please her, I get up again, go and open the window, but close it again without having seen anything.

'It's on the side by the yard!' she shouts this time.

I open the other window, without any further result.

Armand's condition was really abnormal and I became as nervous as her. At a certain moment, she buried her face in the pillow and started sobbing spasmodically.

It was then that, not knowing what else to do, I caught sight of a hammer near the bed. I took it and I struck Armande on the head.

Then I saw a knife and I plunged it into her neck.

After that I did not feel well. I was afraid of staying alone. I went out of the room, and I woke my mother, who was sleeping on the ground floor. I asked her to light a fire, in order to prepare a herbal tea to fortify myself.

'What's happened?' my mother asked, looking at me.

And, as I replied evasively, she pushed open the door of the room, went up to Armande and bent over her.

The hammer was still there. I could not look away from it. My hand grasped it and I struck, exactly as I had struck Armande, and then I took the knife and thrust it into my mother's neck.

I was not at all well. At first I went down to the kitchen and I drank some mint brandy. Afterwards, I fell onto my knees and I prayed for a long time in front of the crucifix.

I could not resign myself to leaving the two women that I loved in the condition in which they were. I went back upstairs, and, all alone, I laid out the corpses and stretched out their bodies under the blankets.

Then I placed a crucifix on the turned-back sheet, and sprigs of boxwood in their ice-cold hands. Finally, I put a mask of Beethoven and a mask of Baudelaire on the bodies.

I always claimed that my mother resembled the mask of Baudelaire. I always felt it, even when I was little.

It was also when I was little, at four or four-and-a-half years old, that I saw a sow being killed, first by a hammer blow to the skull, then by plunging a knife into its neck; I did the same with Armande and with my mother.

I left the house, the door of which I closed again. The day before, when I had already decided to go and serve my two years in prison in Brussels, I had left a suitcase containing some clothes in the left luggage office of the Gare du Nord.

In the morning I collected it and I took the train to Belgium...

At this point the coincidence is going to be amazing. It is easy to believe that neither Deblauwe nor Danse could suffer the fate of ordinary murderers.

Deblauwe, sought after by all police forces, is sitting peacefully in prison, at Saint-Étienne, where it is a miracle that he has been found again.

Danse, scarcely has he alighted in Brussels, goes to a lawyer. He has only one question to put, a question that causes a drop of sweat, caused by agony, to appear on his forehead.

'I have just killed my mother and my mistress, in France,' he admits under the guarantee of professional secrecy. 'Has French law the right to demand my extradition?'

What happens then? Is the lawyer absent-minded? Is it Danse who does not understand his explanations well and who omits to declare his Belgian nationality?

In Belgium, the death penalty does not exist and a murderer has only one concern: to save his head.

'Tell me! Can they require my extradition?'

WELL, THEY CANNOT. DANSE, ARRESTED IN BELGIUM, AND BEING A BELGIAN SUBJECT, WILL BE JUDGED IN BELGIUM FOR THE CRIMES HE HAS COMMITTED IN FRANCE.

He does not understand it in this way. The lawyer expressed himself badly and simply advised him to give himself up. So he's out in the streets, haunted by the prospect of the guillotine.

However, he goes first to the police.

'I am Hyacinthe Danse, sentenced in absentia in 1926, to two years in prison. I have come to serve these two years...'

At Boullay, the bodies of the two women have not yet been discovered. The policeman looks in surprise at his strange client, makes a few phone calls and finally declares, 'I'm sorry but I cannot deal with your request. The offence of blackmail, with which you were charged in 1926, is covered by the statute of limitations...'

They refuse to arrest him, to put him in prison! So there he is out on the streets, not knowing what else to do, still with the nightmare of the guillotine.

He takes the train for Liège the following morning, wanders round his home town, looks at all the familiar places again, his former shop, the Saint-Servais college, and the house where he spent his childhood.

There is still no talk in the newspapers of the drama at Boullay, and he will say later:

'After this pilgrimage to the places that were dear to me, I felt the need to take confession. I went to the retreat house of the Jesuit Fathers, the rue Xhovémont, where I knew I would find the Reverend Father Haut, my former teacher. I took a taxi. I told the driver to wait for me at the door.

'They first had me go into the parlour and the R.F. Haut came, listened to my story of the drama, and then judged that I was not in a sufficiently favourable state of mind to make a valid confession.

'As I appeared exhausted to him, he took me to the refectory and went to look for a bottle of beer. He poured me a glass, which I drank. After a few moments, he leaned over to pour me another glass.

'It was then that I took my revolver out of my pocket and that I fired, because I suddenly remembered all that the R.F. Haut had made me suffer when I was his pupil.

'He got the first bullet in the head and he fell on his knees. I fired a second, and a third time and, holding his hands to his stomach, he collapsed. Then, I fired the other bullets randomly, and I left before anybody came, found my taxi again and ordered the driver: "Take me to the Law Courts!"

'There, I demanded to see a judge or some prosecutor and I told the whole truth.

'For ten years, the R.F. Haut was also my confessor. When he died, he was almost sixty-years old.

'I suddenly remembered what he had made me suffer...' Danse will declare, and, even before asking for a lawyer, he will demand an assessment of his mental state.

For months, he will prove to be the most fantastic of defendants, choosing a lawyer and then, a few days later, throwing him out of his cell, threatening to strangle a defence lawyer appointed by the court, and arguing step by step with the specialists on insanity who are given the responsibility of examining him.

Being shut up, he resembles more than ever an aggressive animal and, eight days before the trial, they are forced to give him a new lawyer, whom he refuses to see.

Then on the day before the Assizes, this lawyer has an idea, takes the train to Paris, and turns up at the office of Maurice Garçon to whom he declares, 'Knowing him as I do, Danse will refuse tomorrow to let himself be defended. Well, he must be defended! I have thought of something... Haunted by ideas of greatness, he will be flattered that a respected member of the Paris Bar puts himself out for him and he will let him speak...'

And that is what happened! With, however, one strange detail. The trial lasted from Monday to Saturday. Now, on the Thursday and Friday, Maurice Garçon absolutely had to plead a case in Paris.

'What shall we do, if my turn to plead comes when I'm not there?' he asks.

'Have no fear. Your turn won't come before Saturday. The Liège lawyer is sure of it.'

'Yet… there are only very few witnesses to hear and…'

'I repeat that you've nothing to fear. When it's the defence's turn to speak, *I will keep talking till you arrive…*'

He did it! Consequently, I was going to write 'heroically', he talked for the whole day on Friday, in order to drag out the trial until Saturday and to allow Maurice Garçon to get there.

During this time, Hyacinthe Danse was writing in careful handwriting, decorating the letters with arabesques, the following poem:

THE DESIRED ONE

I

Knock! Knock! Knock! – Who's knocking at the door?
'Go, poet, and open your door;
   And look!
It's Happiness, near your home!
He wants to enter, beneath your roof!'

'Bah! Just leave the door:
All my joys are dead!…'

II

Knock! Knock! Knock! – Who's knocking at the door?
'Go, poet, open your door;
Come and see:
You can see, passing by, in the evening,

The bright face of Hope!'
'Ah! Just leave the door:
My hope is dead!'

III

Knock! Knock! Knock! – Who's knocking at the door?
'Who goes there? Who makes all that noise?
And who on earth dares open my closed door?'

'Quick! Quick! Defend the door!
Courage, poet, and be strong:
Death is seen entering your home!…'

'Finally…Close the door,
For fear that he will not leave!'

– *G. Hyacinthe Danse*
(A. Montaigle)

He had just been sentenced to forced labour for life and he was able to allow himself the luxury of writing some verses on death: *he was sure, from then on, of not dying!*

Does he remember, in his prison in Louvain, the little girls in poor health who, under the gas lamps ringed with blue, during the war, whispered to us strange stories punctuated by hysterical laughter?

Does he remember the Danse of the patriotic songs and comic refrains? The aggressive Danse of *Nanesse* and the Wise Man of Boullay-les-Trous?

Does he remember having written, in *Savoir*, where he interviewed himself: 'My greatest pleasure? To look a fool in the eyes of an idiot.'

That pleasure, at least, he spoiled. During the six months for the preparation of his case, he grimaced, threatened in vain, and gave free rein to the craziest imaginings.

'My father was syphilitic!' he yelled at the Assizes.

It was established that this was false.

'My mother took morphine!'

And this was also false.

'I have always been haunted by the incident of the sow that I saw killed with a hammer and then a knife, in the same way that I killed Armande and my mother…'

But the R.F. Haut?

'I'm a necrophiliac!'

He is going to itemise all his vices, in a self-satisfied way, with a sidelong glance, to assure himself of the effect produced. He has already managed to replace the guillotine by the prison. All that would be left to do is replace the prison by a nursing home.

'Paranoiac!' Maurice Garçon will plead.

And Danse becomes restless, anxious, suspicious, finding that it is not enough. Doubtless, if it were possible for him, if it could get results, he would eat excrement, right there in front of the jurors, who would have no choice but to take him for a genuine madman.

'Paranoiac, perhaps, but responsible for his actions!' decide the experts.

A partial success, all in all, as his head is still fixed to his shoulders by a neck of pink rolls of fat!

I had a grandmother who, when one told her stories, in the hope of surprising her, was content just to sigh, 'Really, the things people do!'

At Louvain, Danse writes more and more abstruse poems. The Two Brothers died without having quite murdered their mother, who took the precaution of dying before them. Little K..., wearing only one shoe, hung himself in the doorway of the church of Saint-Pholien and the Fakir, who had taught him to stuff his nose with cocaine, died of red wine, through lack of money, in a Parisian hospital.

Tejalda, an employee of the Post Office, a society dancer, torturer of mature women, is no more than a name in criminal annals while they are bombing Madrid, and Deblauwe is in the penal colony.

Who knows if some independent cabinetmaker isn't occupying again the premises of the *caque*?

Finally I took my grandmother to the cemetery. She was so withered that a child's coffin would have sufficed.

'*Really, the things people do!*'

She said that of aeroplanes, submarines, short hair, electric stoves, and I don't know what else!

Perhaps it was a form of admiration? Perhaps also she simply wanted to say, 'What's the point?'

Or else, 'Just for the sake of change!'

What remains of these memories and of us? We were, in troubled times – but aren't we all? – a small group of lads turning over ideas that were as dangerous as bombs and coming close to precipices without knowing it. We resorted to semi-darkness, to faded finery and death's heads to make ourselves feel afraid and we drank to feel crazier. We addressed God the Father and Satan intimately, suppressing a shudder, and we made love with Charlotte to persuade ourselves that love was something disgusting.

That did not prevent life from flowing on, like the Meuse, rising and falling, nor us from getting married, nor did it prevent children from being born, more or less serious diseases from breaking out, hopes and discouragements, difficulties at the end of the month or comforting little dinners.

Little K... the Fakir... Deblauwe... Tejalda... the Two Brothers... Danse and his mother, and in addition Armande of the rue du Caire...

You could draw up some statistics to find out if we have had a better or worse lot than the others, and if we have had a narrow escape. But then it would be necessary to take everything into account, set up columns not only with the murderers and suicides, the murderers and the victims, but in addition the savings account books, the stomach aches, the bouts of pneumonia and miscarriages, the great hopes and little disappointments...

A considerable amount of work!

Impossible work at the present time, since, of that small group in the past, only a certain number of us remain and some more will be scrapped.

I think about the last one who will survive...

But no! He will probably look at the young ones of that time murmuring, '*The things people do!*'

For, when all is said and done, it's all horribly banal.

Notes

1. The office of the German commander (Kommandant – German) during the period of the German occupation of Belgium.
2. *Uhlan* is a German term derived from Polish *ulan* and is applied to any of a body of Prussian light cavalry, originally modelled on Tatar lancers.
3. Some French dictionaries also incorporate general knowledge and function as encyclopaedias.
4. The name implies a square area. In Liège it refers nowadays to a specific area of the city.
5. A stock character in a series of comedy films.
6. '*La Marseillaise*' is the French national anthem, '*La Brabançonne*' the Belgian national anthem and '*La Madelon*' is a soldiers' drinking song about a whore.
7. An insult to the German Kaiser Wilhelm is implied.
8. Albert I was king of Belgium during the First World War; Ferdinand Foch (1851–1929) was a French general during the First World War; Georges Clemenceau (1841–1929) was a French politician.
9. André Tardieu (1876–1945), French politician.
10. Raymond Nicolas Poincaré (1860–1934), French politician and president from 1913 to 1920.
11. Common name for the French Intelligence Service.
12. A follower of Jansenism, a Christian movement of the seventeenth and eighteenth centuries, which emphasised moral rigour and asceticism.
13. The Red Donkey (French).
14. A traditional drinking song about the monks of Saint Bernard, with some bawdy elements.
15. The Agile Rabbit (French), presumably an example of the sort of 'Montmartre-style cabaret' referred to earlier.
16. Paul Verlaine (1844–96), French poet.
17. '*La caque*', meaning 'the herring barrel', was probably chosen as the name for their meeting place to suggest how tightly everyone was packed together, like herrings in a barrel.
18. Popular version of a medieval work on alchemy and magic. The author was known in Latin as Albertus Magnus.
19. This is probably an allusion to the courtyard called Le Cour de Miracles near the church of Notre Dame de Paris, where beggars abandon their fake infirmities and 'the lame walk and the blind see'.
20. One of a series of cartoon comic adventures about three rather grotesque companions who became involved in various unlikely situations. Their name, 'Pieds-Nickelés', suggests something like 'layabouts'. This particular adventure sees them involved with gangsters.

21. La Légia is the name of a small tributary of the Meuse, which it meets in the city of Liège. 'The Fervent City' ('*La Cité Ardente*', French) is a common epithet of the city.

22. Henry Ardel (also known as Henri Ardel) was a popular author of the period.

23. Girolamo Savonarola (1452–98), Italian Dominican priest and religious and political reformer.

24. Jules Joseph Bonnot (1876–1912) was a notorious French anarchist and leader of a gang that robbed banks, murdering people in the process. He was shot as he was about to be arrested.

25. Philosophical work by Friedrich Nietzsche (1844–1900).

26. François Villon (1431–after 1463), French poet.

27. In French, 'La Police Judiciaire' and 'La Sûreté Génerale' respectively.

28. Tanagra is a type of terracotta figurine, dating mainly from the fourth and third centuries BC, named after the ancient Greek city in Boeotia.

29. 'La Thébaïde' is the French rendering of the name of the desert place near Thebes in Egypt to which Christians withdrew. It has come to signify a deserted place, and hence profound solitude.

30. Knowledge or a body of knowledge (French).

31. In the original French this is of course four (for *paix*).

32. Aristide Briand (1862–1932), French politician and winner of the Nobel Peace Prize in 1926.

Biographical note

Georges Simenon was born in 1903 in Liège, Belgium, the eldest son of Désiré Simenon, an insurance clerk, and his wife Henriette. Due to his father's ill health he was forced to abandon his studies at the age of sixteen, and worked as a baker and a bookseller before becoming a journalist at the *Gazette de Liège*.

Simenon published his first novel, *Au Pont des Arches*, in 1921 under the pseudonym 'G. Sim'. In 1921 his father died and in 1922 he moved to Paris with Régine Renchon, whom he had met through the group of artists and bohemians known as '*la caque*'; they married in 1923. In Paris Simenon published numerous short stories and novels under many different pen names; he began writing the famous Commissaire Maigret novels in 1931, writing nineteen in the space of three years, to be followed by a further fifty-eight later in his life.

Simenon continued to live and write in France during its occupation in the Second World War. Following the war there were unfounded rumours that he had collaborated with the Germans, and in 1945 he moved to Canada, then the United States. In New York he met Denyse Ouimet, with whom he began an affair; a day after he divorced Régine in June, 1950, he married Denyse and moved with her to Connecticut, where he lived for the next five years, until he moved with his family to the South of France in 1955 and eventually to Lausanne, Switzerland.

The final Maigret novel was published in 1972, and in 1973 Simenon announced that he was retiring; until the end of his life, he wrote largely autobiographical non-fiction. He died in Lausanne in 1989.

Dr David Carter, born in London in 1945, is a writer, translator and freelance journalist, and currently Professor of

Communicative English at Yonsei University, Seoul. He has also taught at the universities of St Andrews and Southampton, in the UK, and has published on German and French literature, psychoanalysis, aesthetics, film history, drama and applied linguistics. His most recent books include *Georges Simenon* (2003) and *Literary Theory* (2006).

HESPERUS PRESS

Hesperus Press, as suggested by the Latin motto, is committed to bringing near what is far – far both in space and time. Works written by the greatest authors, and unjustly neglected or simply little known in the English-speaking world, are made accessible through new translations and a completely fresh editorial approach. Through these classic works, the reader is introduced to the greatest writers from all times and all cultures.

For more information on Hesperus Press, please visit our website: **www.hesperuspress.com**

ET REMOTISSIMA PROPE

MODERN VOICES

SELECTED TITLES FROM HESPERUS PRESS

Author	Title	Foreword writer
Mikhail Bulgakov	*A Dog's Heart*	A.S. Byatt
Mikhail Bulgakov	*The Fatal Eggs*	Doris Lessing
Anthony Burgess	*The Eve of St Venus*	
Colette	*Claudine's House*	Doris Lessing
Marie Ferranti	*The Princess of Mantua*	
Beppe Fenoglio	*A Private Affair*	Paul Bailey
F. Scott Fitzgerald	*The Popular Girl*	Helen Dunmore
F. Scott Fitzgerald	*The Rich Boy*	John Updike
Graham Greene	*No Man's Land*	David Lodge
Franz Kafka	*Metamorphosis*	Martin Jarvis
Franz Kafka	*The Trial*	Zadie Smith
D.H. Lawrence	*Wintry Peacock*	Amit Chaudhuri
Rosamond Lehmann	*The Gipsy's Baby*	Niall Griffiths
Carlo Levi	*Words are Stones*	Anita Desai
André Malraux	*The Way of the Kings*	Rachel Seiffert
Katherine Mansfield	*In a German Pension*	Linda Grant
Katherine Mansfield	*Prelude*	William Boyd
Vladimir Mayakovsky	*My Discovery of America*	Colum McCann
Luigi Pirandello	*Loveless Love*	
Françoise Sagan	*The Unmade Bed*	
Jean-Paul Sartre	*The Wall*	Justin Cartwright
Bernard Shaw	*The Adventures of the Black Girl in Her Search for God*	Colm Tóibín
Leonard Woolf	*A Tale Told by Moonlight*	Victoria Glendinning